STORIES FROM

THE HEARTLAND

1/31/18

STORIES FROM THE HEARTLAND

BY

BOB PERRY

Stories from the Heartland

Copyright © 2017 by William Robert Perry

Contents

JOSEPHINE KNEW

Cindy's early life had been like that of a princess with three protective older brothers doing their best to spoil her. The affection she received from her family extended beyond the household to aunts, uncles, cousins, and grandparents. On both sides of her family, she had been the first girl born in two generations. A little girl's life could not have been happier.

In fourth grade, however, her magical bubble of happiness burst. Her enchanted youth seemed to unravel into a different reality. One day the teacher presented a lesson on the modern family and asked Cindy a question for which she did not know an answer. The question was one she had never even considered. She was unaware it had any application in her life.

The teacher asked, "What's it like to be adopted, Cindy?"

Cindy remembered the question taking her breath away. It did not seem real to her. The teacher realized her mistake immediately, but it was too late. At recess, other kids played as if the world was normal, but Cindy felt as if everything had changed. Confusion and doubt filled her afternoon walk home. If she is not Cindy Abernathy, who is she?

Her mother greeted her with a plate full of cookies and a cup of hot cocoa when a sobbing Cindy walked into the kitchen.

"Mrs. Smith called from school," her mother began.

"Am I adopted?" Cindy asked pitifully.

Her mother sat in the kitchen chair and pulled Cindy onto her lap, wrapping her arms tightly around her as she answered, "Yes dear."

Cindy's tears soaked into her mother's shoulder for several minutes. Once she regained her composure, Cindy had a long conversation with her mother and learned about the beginnings of a life, which she could not possibly remember.

The Abernathys wanted a fourth child, and Cindy became a blessing they would always cherish. The family received a call on a Friday that a baby needing a family had been born in a neighboring state. They drove through the night to be there, and brought her home on a Sunday. She became their Cindy.

"The boys know?" Cindy asked.

Her mother nodded but adamantly declared her father and brothers only thought of Cindy as their daughter and sister. Her mother had planned to talk with Cindy about the adoption next summer, when they could have some girl time, while the boys would be at basketball camp.

Their conversation helped relieve some of Cindy's uncertainty from earlier in the day, but something in her was different that she would not understand for many years. Turning twelve for Cindy was difficult, as is the case with many young girls. She went through several stages of rebellion, experimentation, and angst that goes along with growing up. When Cindy attended college, she hit her stride, however. Just when she believed her college career could not be better, she met Jim.

Cindy had boyfriends before and even believed herself to be in love a few times, but no one had ever been like Jim. A few months of dating grew into an engagement. Three months after graduation, Cindy Abernathy became Cindy Wilson. Her life was great. Jim understood everything about her—often better than she understood herself. She could talk to him about anything, and, of course, she told him about her adoption. The adoption did not matter to Jim, and more importantly, it did not matter to her anymore, either. Thanksgiving and Christmas were alternated between the Abernathy family and the Wilson family. Cindy found herself firmly a part of both families.

Her adoption was unspoken and nearly forgotten, until the wonderful day she learned she was going to have Jim's baby. Both families were ecstatic with joy, but no one seemed happier than Jim. It was in the seventh month of her first pregnancy when a friend suggested it might be valuable to know more about her biological past. Cindy was resistant at first, but Jim agreed, and her doctor confirmed it "wouldn't hurt" to know more about her family medical history. Cindy reluctantly decided to investigate her past.

It had been years since she had thought much about her adoption. As a teenager, she fantasized that maybe she was special somehow and that her parents were someone famous or perhaps there were extraordinary circumstances involved. As a mature and practical mother-to-be, Cindy understood the reality was probably more sordid. Cindy opened her adoption file before the birth of her first child to learn her biological mother's name was Josephine.

The woman had several last names through the years and still lived in the same rather unimportant Midwestern city where Cindy had been born. Cindy was apathetic about the woman but was now somewhat uneasy at even knowing her name.

Cindy's first child was a beautiful girl followed by two rambunctious boys. Jim proved to be as good a father as he was a husband. By the time Cindy's daughter turned eighteen, she and Jim were happily worn out with coaching softball, attending little league football games, and going to band concerts. When her daughter left for college, Cindy discovered social media, primarily as a means to keep track of her children—especially her attractive daughter now living away from home at college.

Life had been good to Cindy. As she collapsed into her favorite chair to unwind, she spent a few minutes checking her various social media platforms, spying on her daughter and catching up with old friends from college. This night an unexpected friend request caused her heart to skip. A message from a woman she did not know named Josephine, from the city where she had been born, stared at her. Cindy looked at the request for almost an hour. She investigated as much as she could to identify this stranger. She did not learn much but believed Josephine might be the woman who had abandoned her forty-two years earlier.

For two weeks, Cindy did not respond to the request but did not delete it either. For most of her life, her adoption was a repressed memory—something she had successfully ignored. Now, this friend request confronted her every night and haunted her thoughts. Cindy's emotions ranged from wanting to ignore the woman, to giving her a piece of her mind for abandoning her those many years ago. In the end, the curiosity to know nagged at her.

Cindy finally confided to the one person she believed would understand, Jim. She hoped he could give her a definitive answer to ignore, accept, or—even meet this woman. Jim had no answers but pledged his support whatever she chose to do. Jim knew, before Cindy perhaps, that her inquisitive nature would eventually win. She accepted the friend request and now had Josephine in her social media life.

For many weeks, that was the extent of the contact. Cindy made no overtures, and Josephine remained a silent social media acquaintance. It was Cindy's birthday, and she read messages left by her many well-wishing friends when she saw a single line posted by Josephine that said, "Hope your life is always happy."

Hope your life is always happy, Cindy thought to herself. What did that mean? Out of the hundreds of messages from friends that were more thoughtful, or clever, or insightful, this one stuck in her mind.

After a few days, Cindy typed, "Thank you."

A message followed saying, "You're welcome."

"Do I know you?" Cindy replied a day later.

Josephine answered in a few minutes, "No."

"Should I?"

"I don't know."

"Are you my mother?" Cindy finally asked.

"I think so," Josephine confirmed.

The last message stunned Cindy. Josephine sent a few more messages asking if things were okay, but Cindy could not bring herself to answer. She finally showed the messages to Jim.

"What are you going to do?" Jim asked.

I want you to tell me! Cindy thought to herself. You should be objective. You know me better than anyone. Why can't you tell me what to do?

"I don't know," Cindy finally whimpered.

"What do you want to do?" Jim replied.

Cindy sighed, "What do you think I should do?"

Jim hugged her as he said, "I have no idea, but I'm sure you'll figure it out."

It was several more weeks and near midnight before Cindy messaged Josephine, "Can we meet?"

In seconds, the response flashed on her screen, "Yes, if you would like to."

The answer came back so quickly it startled Cindy. This woman—a stranger to her—replies at midnight immediately. Has she been stalking her? How did she see the message so quickly? Everything is moving too fast.

The next morning, Cindy agrees to meet the woman who might be her mother. She insists they meet at a hotel in a nearby city away from her home. She's certain the woman knows where she lives, but Cindy does not feel completely comfortable having this woman in her life. Cindy tells Jim she has agreed to meet, and he says he knew she would. They leave the children behind without telling them the purpose of the trip. They do not know anything about this woman's past, and Cindy does not want to expose them to a stranger.

"Are you going to tell her?" Jim asks, as they work out the details of their trip.

Cindy knows exactly what Jim means, and it is the conversation she has dreaded since the minute she agreed to see Josephine.

Cindy needs to tell her mother about the meeting. Not this woman who claims to be her mother, but her real mother and grandmother to her children. The mother that raised her, who took care of her, and who was always able to soothe her pains of growing up into the woman she has become.

Her mother takes the news with the silent dignity Cindy expects. She asks a few questions like: how long have you known, how did she make contact, and do you think this is a good idea? Cindy has no idea if meeting this woman is wise or not but feels compelled to do it anyway. As always, her mother convinces her everything will work out for the best. Cindy gives her mom an extra-long hug and fights back the tears of emotion flooding over her. Her mother smiles graciously, but Cindy cannot help but feel she is somehow betraying her.

Cindy and Jim make the hour-long drive to the lobby of a nice hotel in a nearby city to meet the woman that abandoned her. Cindy wrings her hands anxiously and unconsciously tugs at her wedding ring wishing she had ignored her curiosity to know something that might be better off unknown. They arrive an hour early expecting to wait for the woman. Cindy has a picture from the social media site of the woman on her phone but wonders if she will be able to recognize the stranger in person.

She does not have to wait as a timidly excited voice calls out nervously, "Cindy?"

Cindy quickly recognizes the woman from the picture. The woman is younger than she expects but somehow seems older and more tired than her years. She wears a dress a couple of sizes too small and a few years out of date. Cindy's initial impression is that the clothes are the best the woman has and that she's not accustomed to dressing so formally.

"Josephine?" Cindy answers back.

The woman walks quickly toward her and stops a step away before scooping Cindy into her arms to hug her tightly. Cindy endures the violation of her personal space for a few seconds by standing rigidly. The woman steps back, emotional and unable to speak, which amplifies Cindy's discomfort.

"Did you have a hard time finding this place?" Cindy asks civilly.

"No," Josephine is able to mutter.

"Why don't we find a table in the restaurant?" Jim suggests, in an attempt to break the awkwardness of the meeting. "I'm sure you both have a lot of questions."

Josephine nods, and Jim's sensitivity impresses Cindy. Her pleasant feelings about her husband evaporate when he suggests he has some shopping to do. Jim claims he will rejoin them in an hour, and offers to buy lunch for the two women. Cindy watches helplessly as Jim leaves her alone with this stranger. She knows her husband never shops, particularly in the city. He has abandoned her.

"Thank you so much for meeting me," Josephine says, as she takes a seat.

Cindy looks at her a moment, contemplating a frail list of reasons she has invented to excuse herself, before finally taking a seat across from the stranger.

"I imagine you have questions," Josephine enthusiastically smiles. "I know I do."

Cindy nods politely but is unable to bring herself to ask the only question she has ever really had—why did you give me up?

"Tell me something about yourself?" Josephine coaxes, as she seems undeterred at her daughter's lack of excitement about the meeting.

"There's not much to tell," Cindy shrugs. "I have three older brothers. I graduated from college and got married."

"To Jim?" Josephine interjects.

It had not occurred to Cindy that anyone would ever think that she would be married to anyone but Jim, as she answers, "Yes."

"He seems very nice," Josephine notes.

Cindy can't help smiling as she thinks of how clever her husband has been in leaving her alone with this woman as she answers, "Yes, he is. He's a great—father."

Cindy chokes off her last words as she is uncomfortable talking to this woman about her family. Josephine does not seem offended, and instead, hangs on every word.

"So, you married Jim, and have children?" Josephine asks.

"A girl and two boys," Cindy replies. "Bethany's a junior in college. Brad will graduate from high school next year, and Bart's a sophomore."

"Do you have pictures?" Josephine asks.

Cindy had not thought to bring photographs of her children. She wanted to shelter her children, but then remembers she has a phone filled with pictures. After locating some of the best shots, she hands the device to the woman. Josephine is completely absorbed in studying the children and for a few moments seems to forget her daughter sitting across the table. Cindy takes the time to study this woman more carefully.

Josephine looks out of place. Her clothes were nice enough once, but are a few years past their prime, indicating a lack of taste and affluence Cindy has become accustomed to in her suburban cul-de-sac. Josephine has the stale smell of cigarettes she has tried to camouflage by wearing too much cheap perfume. It is hard for Cindy to tell what the woman's true hair color is, although today's faded ginger color somehow doesn't fit her age. Josephine has done her best to present herself, but at least one of her back teeth is missing, and her hands look as if they are used to hard work. Josephine is more pleasant than Cindy expected, but she suspects the woman's life has not been easy.

"They're just wonderful," Josephine extols, as she continues gawking at the children.

Cindy suddenly finds herself uncomfortable with the woman staring at the pictures of her life. She says, "Yes," as she reaches over and tactfully takes back possession of the phone.

For the next hour, the conversation remains polite but uncomfortable. Cindy picks at a salad, as Josephine gobbles down a sandwich, while continuing a barrage of questions. Cindy learns more about her biological past, but the true question she wants answered eludes her. She discovers Josephine has two grown children—albeit with two different men who were not Cindy's father. Cindy had never entertained the idea she might have siblings beyond her three older brothers, but learns she has a half-sister named Lisa working as a secretary in Virginia. Josephine explains her daughter had been a bright girl and finished a year of college before taking a good job. Her half-brother Tom, had some rough stretches according to Josephine, but now worked construction somewhere in Texas.

Cindy spends more time answering questions than asking, but after the initial awkwardness, begins to feel more comfortable in the conversation. Josephine was seventeen when she had Cindy. The father moved away before she was born and never contacted Josephine again. She heard he was selling condominiums in Florida and had done well for himself. Josephine works as a server at a Waffle House and claims to enjoy the work. She says the tips are good and the people interesting. She bought a house a few years ago and overall seems content with her life.

"There's Jim!" Cindy interrupts, with a muffled exclamation, as she sees her husband meandering up the sidewalk empty-handed from his supposed shopping excursion.

Josephine senses the relief in Cindy's voice. The woman understands she has dominated the conversation and enjoyed the meeting much more than her daughter has. She smiles politely and nods.

Before Jim can join them, Josephine says, "Thank you so much for meeting me. I dreamt of this for—all of your life, but never thought it would happen. There's so much I've wanted to say— but—I suppose I've not said any of it well. Is there any chance we might meet again? Maybe we could be friends and share some more of our past."

"I—I don't think that's a good idea," Cindy sighs.

"Of course," Josephine quickly agrees. "I understand that completely. Again—it was so good to meet you. You don't really know how much it means to me. Really."

"Jim's waiting," Cindy says. "We've got a long trip back."

Josephine nods. Cindy doesn't know how to say goodbye to a woman she never expects to see again. She nods rigidly at Josephine before leaving her at the restaurant table—alone.

"Is everything alright?" Jim asks, as his wife quickly exits the building.

"Yes," Cindy answers in an emotionless daze. "Let's go."

Jim is on the highway before asking, "How did it go?"

Cindy heaves a sigh, "I don't know. It was—it was very strange. I understand that woman gave birth to me, but I—I felt nothing."

"Were you worried?" Jim asks.

"About what?"

"You know," Jim explains. "We've done pretty well. Did she want anything? Did she want to see the kids? A woman like that, who knows what she expects."

"She didn't want anything," Cindy says. "She was nicer than I thought and—very polite—very respectful of my privacy. I have a half-sister and half-brother I didn't know about."

"That's interesting," Jim smiles. "You going to look them up?"

Cindy shakes her head, "I don't see why. I'm not connected to them. It's strange to think I'm an older sister to somebody. I've always been the baby of the family."

Her husband drives farther before asking, "What's really bothering you?"

Jim always has a sense about her when it comes to the important things. She has said little to him as she's tried to put this meeting behind her, but he knows something troubles her.

Cindy frowns, "I can't help but think what my life might have been if she had kept me. I would be the same person, but— everything about me would be different. My brothers—I can't imagine growing up without them. I would have gone to a different school. Who knows if I would have been able to go to college? I certainly wouldn't have gone to our school—I wouldn't have met you. Maybe I'd be working as a secretary with one year of community college on my resume."

Jim grins, but doesn't reply immediately.

"What is it?" Cindy huffs.

"I think I understand, but I believe we were meant to be together," Jim says. "Who knows? Maybe you'd have been my secretary."

Cindy smiles inside at her husband's affirmation about their relationship as she reaches over and touches his hand.

"There's more," Jim surmises. "You're not telling me everything."

Cindy lets the car move farther down the road before saying, "I couldn't do it. I couldn't make myself ask the only question that's really bugged me all these years. Why did she give me up? I know she was young, but I—I can't imagine giving up any of my children like that."

"Life can be hard, I guess," Jim surmises. "Like you said, she was young. Besides, it doesn't look like things have been too prosperous. Maybe she didn't feel like she had options."

"Maybe," Cindy concedes.

"Are you going to ask her?" Jim adds. "Are you going to see her again?"

Cindy thinks for a moment, but feels she has already answered the question in her own mind, "No. I don't see any point. Today was much harder than I thought. I almost regret the meeting, although Josephine was nothing but pleasant. I'm not sure I should have put myself in that situation. I feel badly for putting my mom through it, and I can't see any way I'd expose my children to a past that doesn't matter anymore."

"It's your decision," Jim says supportively. "I'm proud of you though. It took courage to come today."

"I don't know about that," Cindy frowns. "I don't feel very courageous about today. I want to see Mom and our kids. I'm ready for things to return to normal for a while."

For several weeks, Cindy did her best to put Josephine out of her mind. Josephine sent a note of thanks via social media. Cindy did not respond, and Josephine seemed to respect Cindy's desire to end the relationship and did not attempt to contact her again. As Thanksgiving approached, however, Cindy found herself failing to put Josephine's decision to give her up behind her. She fretted for days. Jim knew something was wrong, but didn't interfere. When she planned to invite Josephine to the house the weekend before Thanksgiving, he was not surprised. Josephine, on the other hand, seemed totally shocked and nearly overwhelmed with joy at the opportunity. Cindy made arrangements and regretted her decision almost immediately.

Cindy took pride in her holiday decorations, as her mother always had, but this year she was particularly anxious to make things perfect. She had Jim make reservations at a local hotel for Josephine. It was too long of a trip to make in one day, and Cindy did not feel comfortable having a stranger stay overnight in her house. She would have plenty of support for this meeting. Cindy invited her parents and three brothers. Her daughter was still a few days from Thanksgiving vacation, and she planned to send the boys to stay with friends. She was still uncomfortable subjecting her children to her past—or to Josephine.

Josephine arrived at the bus station wearing the same outfit she wore on their initial meeting, but her hair was tinted a darker shade of muddy brown. Josephine entered Cindy's home nervously, but joyfully. The second meeting was easier for Cindy with help from her family in driving the conversation and answering questions about Cindy's childhood. By the time supper concluded, the entire party became comfortable with the odd reunion. Cindy's brothers even seemed to enjoy recounting some of the old family stories about her childhood deeds and misdeeds.

Cindy observed Josephine relishing every insignificant detail about her childhood. She paid even more attention to her mother, trying desperately to see if her brother's recollections were bothersome to her. Cindy could only imagine what meeting the biological mother must be to the woman she still and forever would consider her real mother. Things went well, and Josephine was an appreciative guest.

It was late in the evening before Cindy's mother said, "I think we better be going, dear." Looking at Cindy, her mother continues, "Don't you think you should drive Josephine to her hotel? I'll cook breakfast tomorrow. Could you possibly bring Josephine by to see my house? That is, if she has the time."

"Of course," Josephine quickly replies. "That would be a lovely gesture. Is it the house where Cindy grew up?"

"Yes," Cindy's mother confirms. "I thought you might want to see where some of these exaggerated stories you've heard about Cindy happened."

"I very much would," Josephine replies.

Cindy expects Jim to drive them, but her mother contrives an excuse for him to help her with a nonsensical project. This forces Cindy to be alone for the first time this evening with Josephine. The joviality of the night evaporates as Cindy drives though the dark night. She endures clumsy silence, as she had during their first meeting. Josephine tries her best to be pleasant, but Cindy has a difficult time relaxing without the support of her family. Cindy parks near the hotel's entrance, anxious about how she will end this evening. She mutters the words, "Goodbye," but Josephine sits in the car silently.

"Are you going to ask me?" Josephine finally sighs.

"Ask what?" Cindy replies, although she knows the answer to the question.

Josephine hesitates, as if collecting her thoughts from a well-rehearsed speech, before saying, "Have you heard of Jochebed?"

Cindy searches her memory about the odd name before saying, "The mother of Moses—from the Old Testament?"

Josephine nods, "She gave up her son, Moses, to Pharaoh's family, but I've always wanted to know what was going through Jochebed's mind. I know why she did it. It was the only way to save her child. Still it must have been so—so hard for her. I know what you really want to ask. Why did I do it? What kind of woman would give up her child?"

"Yes," Cindy bluntly replies. "I've wondered that. Ever since I learned I was adopted, I've felt there's a part of me that's a secret. I've always wanted to know."

Josephine nods her head and smiles strangely, "I've thought about how I would answer that question ever since the day you were born. I always dreamed someday we would meet, and I would try to explain I did it out of love, but I always knew it would be impossible for anyone to really understand."

"Why don't you try?" Cindy suggests.

"I was young when I met your father," Josephine begins. "Way too young, but like most young girls, I didn't believe it at the time. I was only sixteen—his name was Joe. I believed it was so cute to think Joe and Josephine would live happily ever after. Joe was a good talker. He paid attention to me like no one ever had. He was older, more experienced, and I felt like I was finally liberated from the life I thought I was destined to have. He was so nice to me— and I was nice to him. Then I found out I was pregnant—with you. I was scared, but happy. I thought Joe would marry me, and I would finally have a family—a family of my own.

"Joe was not so nice when I told him the news. He wondered how I could be so stupid. After he cooled down, he offered to take me to the clinic. He would take care of everything, and our lives could get back to normal. I made it all the way to the clinic, but by then I thought of you living inside me. I couldn't do it. Joe insisted. He got real mad—called me a lot of names that—I guess I deserved. I didn't always do the right thing when I was younger, but—I finally stood up to Joe like I should have from the start. He left that day, and I never saw him again."

"You said, 'a family of you own,'" Cindy interjects.

Josephine nods, "I was raised in an orphanage—a good Christian one. That's how I knew the story of Moses and his mother. I don't have many memories of any home other than the orphanage. I had some foster homes. I would go for a few weeks and sometimes a few months. I kept thinking I might find a home. Other kids found families, but year in and year out I grew older in the orphanage, and no one wanted me. I didn't know what was wrong with me, but understood something wasn't right or else some family would have adopted me."

"That's terrible," Cindy moans.

"I'm not making excuses," Josephine continues. "But when Joe paid me so much attention, I thought, for the first time, I was special. When I had to return to the orphanage after he left me, I felt hopeless, but had nowhere else to go. I didn't really understand how mean the world could be back then.

"But, the people at the orphanage understood. Looking back, it shouldn't have surprised me, because they knew all about girls in trouble. One of the older women was particularly kind to me. She bragged at how brave I had been not to have the abortion, but talked to me about the realities of having a baby at my age. She questioned how I could possibly support a child in a way that convinced me I couldn't. She told me a newborn—like you—would be easy to match to a family. She promised she would find a good family—one that could take care of you—one that would love you. She said she could find some money for the hospital. Most of all, she told me it would be the best for you."

Josephine smiles and cries as she says, "Tonight has been one of the happiest days of my life. That woman did not lie to me. She did find a family to take care of you—to love you. Look at you now. I could have never done half as much for you."

Cindy does not know how to respond, but it doesn't matter. She's too choked up to speak and can do nothing but look at the woman that until tonight, she feels she really never could know.

"I don't expect you to understand," Josephine whispers. "But I want you to know I'm happy for you. I'm happy for—everything about you."

"I think I understand," Cindy whimpers, as she reaches across the car seat to embrace the woman and hold her tightly.

The two women cry. No words can describe their emotions, but for the first time in her life, Cindy feels connected to something she never knew she missed.

Wiping the tears from her eyes, Josephine says, "When I turned eighteen, I learned my mother who took me to the children's home would never sign the papers that would allow me to be put up for adoption. All those years, I thought the families didn't want me. They couldn't tell me the reason. I always believed I wasn't good enough. I had a hard time when I gave you up. I wanted to go see you in the nursery. I wanted to see what kind of family I was giving you to, but the people at the orphanage talked me out of it. They were right. If I had seen you, I never could have let you go. I couldn't have taken care of you properly, and I'd have been no better than the mother who condemned me to an orphanage for all those years. Putting you with the Abernathys was the best thing I could do. I tried to convince myself of that then, but now I see it was true.

"I would have loved you, but I've had my share of problems. I've made some bad decisions. I've never been any good at picking men. I was better able to take care of my other two kids—they turned out okay—I'm proud of them."

"I would like to meet them sometime," Cindy says.

Josephine looks at her in near disbelief as she says, "They would love that. I've—I've never told them about you. It will be a shock, but—it might explain some things about me to them. I took the job at the Waffle House because the hours were good. The money's better than you think, and for the most part, the people are decent. I've made a good life for myself—I'm content anyhow. I've worked in that restaurant for nearly thirty years. The one thing that got me to work every day was the idea—the fantasy—that someday I might meet you. I played a game where I would try to guess how old you would be and what you might look like. Every once in a while, I'd see a girl, or later a woman, that I thought might be my daughter. They would get extra good service. I knew it was never real, but then—I found you."

"You found me," Cindy cries.

"It's getting late," Josephine says. "I better get to my room."

"I'll see you tomorrow?" Cindy asks.

Josephine smiles and says deliberately, "Your mother did invite me."

"She did," Cindy smiles, as she wipes the tears from her eyes.

Josephine walks around to Cindy's window after getting out of the car and says, "I always knew I did the right thing. I—I guess I hoped more than I knew. Tonight, I know I made a better life for you. I haven't always been as happy as I should, but I can say tonight I'm truly happy—and I'm so glad to know you."

Cindy nods, "My boys will be at the house tomorrow. I want you to meet them."

"That would be nice," Josephine smiles.

"Bethany's still at school," Cindy informs. "Maybe we could come up and see you—around Christmas."

"I can put a tree up," Josephine beams.

As Josephine walks toward the hotel entrance, Cindy cannot take her eyes off the woman. She's confident she'll never be able to think of Josephine as her mother, but still feels a connection to the woman that is hard to put into words. Cindy marvels at how young Josephine was when she made the difficult decision to give her child away. As a mother, Cindy understands she would do anything for her children. Josephine did something much harder than she could ever imagine. The waitress from the Waffle House, this stranger, this person that is now her friend—the mother that she never knew, turns to wave in an unapologetic and enthusiastic way that would have made Cindy uneasy a few hours earlier. Cindy waves back, as a smiling Josephine enters her hotel.

Cindy looks at the spot where Josephine had stood only moments ago. Josephine knew what was best for her child, Cindy thinks to herself. She could have ended her daughter's life for her own convenience, and that of the man she thought she loved, but Josephine knew. She could have tried to keep her child, but understood as a mere child herself she had little to offer the daughter she loved. Josephine always believed she had done the best for her child, but now, after a lifetime of believing, Josephine knew.

THE END

GRANDMA'S HATCHET

"What's this?" I ask, as I carefully remove the strange object hanging from a nail in Grandma Hulsey's kitchen.

I'm not asking as much about what the object is, as to why it's hanging in my grandmother's kitchen pantry. Grandma Hulsey "departed this earth," as the preacher had so eloquently stated in her eulogy, the previous week. I've lived in another state for the last several years and was embarrassed to think it had been over four years since I had visited her. My memories of her were always fond, and I spent many afternoons in Grandma's kitchen as she made me cinnamon toast in the afternoons after school. The kitchen seems smaller somehow but more important than I remember from my childhood, as I help Dad sort through Grandma's few belongings left in the house after the auction.

My father smiles faintly as he reaches out his hand to hold the small hatchet. He grasps the tool and makes a subtle chopping motion.

"There's a story behind this," Dad grins. "Do you remember your grandmother saying, 'Never do a thing halfway'?"

I nod as I think about my grandma kindly scolding me to finish projects and take responsibility by using those exact words.

"This hatchet's the reason why," Dad continues. "Or at least this is the result of a job half done."

"Why is it in the kitchen?" I smirk.

Dad laughs, "You probably remember what a good cook your grandmother was?"

"Sure," I agree, remembering the many pieces of cinnamon toast, cinnamon rolls, and cinnamon crisps I had consumed as a kid. "She always had something sweet, but I particularly remember her green beans."

"Fried okra, mashed potatoes, pot roast," Dad continues. "I can almost smell the bacon in the air. She used it in almost everything. But—when I was a kid, our big treat was fried chicken. No one could fry chicken like my mother. I think she enjoyed watching us eat her cooking as much as she enjoyed eating it herself. Fried chicken was the Sunday special, but sometimes she would cook it if company were coming.

"Your grandma was a farm girl. She was the oldest of eleven, with seven brothers to feed that worked the farm. She woke up every morning at five o'clock to cook for the boys. It's fair to say she got better than most—and I think she enjoyed cooking for people as much as anyone could. When she married and moved to town, I think her poor brothers cried a little. My aunt was an okay cook but nothing like Mom.

"I remember Dad telling the story of the first time they went to the store for groceries after they were married. Mom had always cooked for at least a dozen people, so she bought a fifty-pound bag of flour, not realizing how long that would last for just two people. She never wanted to be without food, and I suspect she routinely had a half-year's supply of groceries in her pantry."

"So," I interrupt. "What does the hatchet have to do with her cooking?"

Dad redirects, "Like I said, she was a farm girl and could never understand people buying a chicken from the grocer. Even after moving to town, she kept chickens in the backyard for eggs and Sunday dinner. Dad grew up in the country, too, and knew how to wring a chicken's neck. As a boy, I was always mesmerized by his ability to grab a chicken and kill it by popping its head off. It doesn't seem too humane these days, but that's the way they put food on the table back then.

"There was a gospel meeting in town. Your grandparents never missed a chance to go to any meeting in a three-county area, but this preacher was staying in town. All the traveling preachers knew about your grandma's cooking and never turned down an opportunity to come for an early supper. It was a Tuesday, and Grandpa had invited the preacher to the house for a meal. Dad got caught late at the store, which meant Mom had to kill and clean the chicken. She was frantic, and as soon as my sister Rebecca came home from school, Mom gave the order for her to wring the chicken's neck.

"I'd have done it, but Mom thought I was too young. Rebecca was none too keen on the idea, but when she refused, Mom insisted she needed to learn how. Rebecca was fearful of chickens to begin with, but she was more afraid of Mom. I remember watching her like it was yesterday. Rebecca tried to sneak up on the chicken, but wouldn't grab hold of it until Mom yelled at her to get the job done. After that scolding, Rebecca was mad enough to do it—well, almost. She got hold of the chicken and halfway popped it. She managed to break the chicken's neck, but didn't quite kill it.

That chicken squawked around the backyard chasing my sister, with its head hanging to one side at a ninety-degree angle. Rebecca finally gained her wits enough to make it back inside.

"I can't really recall who was more upset: Rebecca, my mom, or the chicken. Mom shouted for Rebecca to finish the job, Rebecca cried that she couldn't do it, and the chicken was making more of a racket as it flopped around the backyard with its neck dangling to one side. Mom recovered her senses and claimed they could wait it out. The chicken had to die eventually. The chicken had another plan and seemed to be getting stronger and louder by the minute. We learned Mom didn't know how to wring a chicken's neck any more than Rebecca! I remember I was entertained, but I'd never seen my sister or mother cry as much as they did that day. Finally, Mom called the store and told my father he had to come home.

"Dad showed up in his suit and tie completely confused and somewhat perturbed at the interruption to his day. He quickly caught the crazy chicken and finished the job my sister had started. Dad didn't say anything, but handed the chicken to my mother and retreated to work. Mom fried the chicken, and it was delicious as always, but I still remember the pathetic look on her face. I think that was the only meal she ever cooked that she didn't enjoy."

"And the hatchet?" I prod.

"Dad never said a word to my mom or sister about the chicken incident," my father grins. "But, the next day, he went to the hardware store and bought Mom this small hatchet with a note saying, 'This might help next time.' Mom quit keeping chickens not long after that and decided the grocer was better suited to supply her than her backyard. She kept the hatchet hanging in the kitchen pantry, however, and would always point to it when admonishing Rebecca or any of the other kids to finish a job. She'd say, 'Halfway doing a job is like leaving a chicken with its neck broke. Never do a thing halfway!'"

Dad hands the hatchet back to me as he says, "Take this home. Your grandmother was right. 'Never do a thing halfway.'"

I hold the hatchet in my hand and stare at it for a moment. I had not taken the good advice my grandma had given to me so many times. I started many grandiose plans and finished very few of them. I'm ashamed and regretful. I had been too distracted with my selfish amusements to take a weekend to visit her before she died. I took her words and her life for granted. Now she's gone, and I'm left with the haunting memory of her well-intentioned advice. I fight back tears as I look up at my dad. He's not judging me, but knows I've not done as much with my life as I could.

"Your grandmother had another saying," Dad says, as he puts a hand on my shoulder.

I sniffle. "It's never too late to start doing the right thing?"

Dad nods, "That's the saying she attributed to me. I was a slow starter in life, too. She told me one time that you can't change your past, but you can start living for today and make your tomorrow whatever you want it to be. You were special to your grandmother. She'd want you to have this hatchet—and to remember her."

I rub my eyes and take a deep breath as I examine my inheritance and manage to say, "I'll try."

THE END

Cletus Callaway

Cletus Callaway loved a good scheme. What he didn't like was hard work: even when his plans caused him considerably more effort than actual labor would have. One time, Cletus saw a Philco® radio in the window of the S&H Green Stamp® store for eleven books of stamps.

For a single man in 1954, collecting eleven books full of S&H Stamps® seemed a formidable task. Cletus was never one deterred in his efforts to beat the system, however. After two months, he barely had more than three books, but he really wanted that radio. Cletus decided he would be hard pressed to collect enough stamps on his own so he started loitering around the Conoco gas station across the road from my store soliciting stamps from other customers, sometimes trading a cigarette or a piece of gum for their stamps. It took Cletus four months of spending every spare moment at the gas station, but he finally traded for his radio. It never occurred to him the radio was a plug-in model, and his cabin on the Barley's place had no electricity.

Old-lady Barley's house did have electricity, and she fancied a radio. She bought Cletus's S&H Green Stamp® Philco® for two dollars. Cletus was satisfied with his windfall, although I had watched him from the front of my store give out at least four dollars' worth of cigarettes as he collected his stamp books—never mind the hours he spent trying to talk the gas station customers out of their stamps. I figured he could have spent his time picking up pop bottles along the highway and had enough money left over for five radios—even if he didn't have a way to plug any of them in. Overall, Cletus was a pleasant enough fellow, just not too bright or too industrious. Cletus Callaway did love his schemes, however.

Cletus worked—or at least had been on the payroll—at the Barley's farm for eighteen years. Orphaned during the later years of the Great Depression, he came to work for Mr. Barley when he was barely twelve. Mr. Barley was demanding, as most farmers tend to be, but was fair to the boy and even took a liking to him. Cletus had one living relative, his Uncle Cecil. Cecil Callaway was more of a schemer than his nephew and considerably more successful, to the point of being called a cheat and thief by some. No one exactly knew Cecil's occupation, but I always found him to be a fairly shiftless character and not prone to any physical labor. Cecil would be gone for months at a time and only occasionally returned to check on his nephew. No one seemed to mind his absences, and Mr. and Mrs. Barley more or less took care of Cletus.

Cletus was too young for the war, and with farm hands hard to come by, he was somewhat helpful to the Barleys. A few years after the war, when Cletus turned twenty, Mr. Barley suffered a stroke that slid into pneumonia that even Penicillin couldn't cure. The farm needed some work in the later years of Mr. Barley's life. The widow Barley, who Cletus always called old lady Barley, was left with a substantial piece of property as her inheritance, but with no other help than her scheming farm hand, the place had fallen into disrepair. Old-lady Barley was a feisty woman who gave the appearance of being stern, shrewd, and demanding, but in reality, she had a soft spot for Cletus and was not able or willing to give him the type of supervision he needed to keep the place maintained. I'd see Cletus a couple of times each month when he would come to the hardware store. You couldn't say we were friends, since I was several years his senior, but we were always friendly.

The front door bell interrupts my morning paper indicating a customer entering the store. I look up to see Cletus sauntering lazily down the aisle in no particular hurry—or so it seemed.

"What can I do you for?" I cheerfully greet, as is my custom.

Cletus shakes his head ever so slightly as he replies, "The old lady thinks the garden gate needs a coat of paint."

"A coat of paint?" I chirp. "That place needs more than a coat of paint. When are you going to do something about that south fence? It's been down on the ground for a year. You can't run any cattle or keep anything out of that pasture until you get that fixed."

"It's on my list," Cletus grins.

"When are you going to get around to actually doing something about that list?" I chide. "Your fence is down, and you haven't planted a crop in three years. The barn's about to fall over when all you'd have to do is brace the rafters and paint it every once and a while."

"Don't you worry about it," Cletus smiles.

"It's not my worry," I frown, as I fetch a gallon of white paint from the shelf. "It's just a shame to see what's become of that place. You're the hired hand. Isn't it your job to keep the place productive? Is the widow Barley that hard up? You're right it's not my business, but it does seem a shame."

"Old lady Barley has all the money she'll ever need," Cletus boasts. "She don't need that farm to produce so why do I need to kill myself? I got a plan and doin' as little to that place as possible is part of it."

"Don't seem very honest," I mutter. "The Barleys have been good to you. Seems like a little effort on your part would be the right thing."

Cletus grins strangely as he replies, "Don't worry your head about it. The less work I do the more money she'll have to leave that nephew of hers over in Chickasha."

"I'd just be careful," I sigh. "One of these days the widow may wake up to how little you're doing to keep up the place."

"I can handle the old lady," Cletus huffs as he takes his paint and shuffles out the door.

A few weeks go by—maybe more than a month—before I see Cletus back in town. He managed to paint a part of widow Barley's garden gate, but never finished the job. Typical of Cletus, he painted the easy to reach places and abandoned the project into a mess. Weeds continued to grow up, nearly devouring the place that Mr. Barley had worked so hard to create. The widow Barley was becoming feeble and rarely ventured out of her house. I wonder if she understands how much the place has gone downhill. Cletus had let the once prosperous farm deteriorate to where it would be hard to even sell at a fair price.

I see Cletus leaning against the fender of a black Cadillac filling up at the Conoco station across the road. The car shines, even though a fine film of dust covers the chrome grill, bumper, and hubcaps. I first think Cletus is hustling green stamps again, but as I watch closer, I see he's in a more serious conversation.

It takes a minute to recognize the driver of the black Cadillac is Cecil Callaway, Cletus's uncle. Cecil had been gone from town for over a year and few missed him. Cletus nods his farewell, as his uncle sprinkles him with gravel when he speeds away from the Conoco station. It's a slow day at the hardware store, and I'm caught spying on Cletus as he waves at me from across the road. I acknowledge him as he slowly walks across the road.

"Was that Cecil?" I ask, as Cletus enters the store.

"Yip," Cletus replies.

"Didn't know he was back in town," I shrug.

"He's not," Cletus reveals. "Just stopped by to talk some business."

"Business?" I quiz. "What kind of business?"

"That's none of your concern," Cletus scolds.

"You're right," I quickly apologize.

Cletus, however, is determined to tell me about his uncle as he says, "If you've got to know, Cecil's into a land development project over in Lawton. He's got investors and everything. He's buyin' up old farmhouses and building neighborhoods for the soldiers stationed at Fort Sill."

"He's not asking you to invest?" I ask.

Cletus grins, "Uncle Cecil's a little rich for my blood. Did you see that Cadillac he's driving? He's doin' great. We might do some business someday, if Cecil will have me."

"You be careful with anything your Uncle Cecil tries to talk you into," I warn. "He's your kin and all, but he's got a reputation as a rascal."

"It takes money to make money," Cletus reasons. "You might call Cecil a rascal, but the way I see it, he's just being shrewd."

Eager to avoid a debate about Cecil Callaway's character, I ask, "What can I do you for today?"

Cletus frowns, "I need a container of DDT. Old lady Barley's scared of spiders and has been after me to spray the place."

"I'll go see what I got," I reply. As I move to the back of the store to check my stock, I ask, "When are you going to finish painting that garden gate?"

"I don't know," Cletus shrugs.

"How about that south fence or the barn?" I press. "That place is falling down around you. With a little effort, it could be a nice farm."

Cletus smirks, "Old lady Barley don't get out of the house these days, so what does she care? She's got plenty of money to live on. Why should I knock myself out for nothing?"

"It's your job?" I retort.

"Don't you worry about me and old-lady Barley," Cletus says. "Who knows? After she's gone, that place might make an attractive investment."

I stop looking for the can of DDT to study Cletus for a moment before asserting, "You mean for someone like your Uncle Cecil? Is that your plan? Let the place get so dilapidated that it sells for pennies on the dollar—to your uncle?"

"I wouldn't say that's a plan," Cletus defends. "I just don't see that killing myself to make the Barley's place more valuable is in my best interest. Uncle Cecil's a clever fella. If he buys it for a good price, he'll be willing to pay good money to put it back into shape."

"Payin' you?" I huff.

"That'd make sense," Cletus surmises.

"Don't seem completely honest of you," I complain.

Cletus smiles, "Don't see why you'd care. I'll need plenty of supplies when the time comes."

"Mrs. Barley would pay to have the work done now," I inform. "And by the man she's already got on her payroll."

Cletus takes his scolding but doesn't defend himself against my accusation.

"You need to be careful with your Uncle Cecil," I advise. "My experience with guys like him is that things always work better for them than anybody else."

"Can I just get the DDT and get out of here?" Cletus huffs.

"I can't help you today, Cletus," I apologize. "I'm out. I'll have a truck in Friday and can get it to you then."

"That'll have to do," he frowns. "I'll come back Friday afternoon."

As Cletus leaves the store, I feel a sense of guilt—not for warning him about his uncle or scolding him for his laziness, but I had slid my last container of DDT out of his sight. I decided, while talking to Cletus, that I need to pay the widow Barley a visit. Delivering the DDT seems like a good excuse to go to her house. It doesn't seem right for Cletus to take advantage of her, and the Barleys had been good customers to me for many years.

The wind blows hot air across my face as I lock up the store for the evening. The worst of summer is over, but there's still plenty of heat in the late afternoon. It's a short trip to the Barley farm down a deeply rutted dirt road. I don't drive by the place much, but it looks worse than I remembered. The fence appears completely down around the entire house. The fields have reverted to sagebrush and don't resemble the carefully plowed fields Mr. Barley had been so proud to plant. As I predicted, the barn has collapsed at the back and appears unusable. Most infuriating to me is that the simple job of painting the poor widow's garden gate has been left undone. Elm trees have grown into the foundation of the house and what would have been an easy job two summers ago now threatens to destroy the house. If Cletus has determined to drive down the value of the property, he has for once succeeded. I knock on the door, dreading this meeting, but feel I owe it to the widow Barley.

"What are you doing here?" Cletus greets, in a whispered tone mixed with anxiousness and anger.

I hold up a paper bag as I reply, "I found a container of DDT after all. Thought I'd drop it by and visit Mrs. Barley."

"Thanks," Cletus says, as he hastily grabs the bag. "The old lady's sleeping, but I'll tell her you came by."

"Who's at the door?" a feeble sounding female voice asks from somewhere in the house.

"Nobody," Cletus shouts back. "It's just Harold from the hardware store dropping off something for the house."

"Have him come in," the woman commands.

Cletus stares at me nervously but does not defy the old woman as he moves slightly to let me step into the front room. The house doesn't look much better on the inside than it does from outside. Mrs. Barley appears thin and frail as she sits in a rocking chair. Cletus's Philco® radio plays music softly in the background. If Mrs. Barley can see me at all, it is faintly in the dark room. She seems to recognize my voice, but her eyes do not focus on me.

"How have you been, Harold?" Mrs. Barley asks. "Have a seat and visit for a while, if you have time."

"I do," I reply, as I slide some old papers cluttering the couch out of the way. "I've closed the store for the day and have a few minutes before I head home."

Cletus takes a chair next to the widow and continues to look anxious about what I might say.

"Time gets away from me," Mrs. Barley claims. "It seems all I do anymore is sit in this chair and listen to the radio."

"Have you been well?" I ask.

Mrs. Barley frowns, "Not as well as I would like, but what good does it do to complain. Cletus, where's your manners? Why don't you fix Harold some tea—or at least some cool water from the well?"

Cletus hesitates to leave before saying, "Yes, ma'am."

As soon as Cletus leaves, I say, "I'm glad you sent Cletus away. I've been wanting to talk to you."

"What's Cletus done now?" Mrs. Barley asks, as she struggles to lean forward in her chair.

"He's not done anything," I reply. "I think that's the problem. Have you seen the condition of your farm lately?"

Mrs. Barley smiles mischievously as she says, "If you haven't noticed, I don't see much of anything these days."

"I didn't mean to be disrespectful," I quickly apologize.

"Harold, I've known you since you were a stock boy at the store and have never thought you had the capacity to be disrespectful. You're worried the old farm's not what it used to be when Mr. Barley was running things."

"Well, yes," I admit.

Mrs. Barley nods, "Things have changed around here that's for sure. I'm pretty much stuck in the house. Cletus moved in about a year ago and does about as much taking care of me as he does the farm."

"My real concern is that Cletus may be purposely letting the property rundown," I assert.

"Why would you think that?" Mrs. Barley asks calmly.

"Everyone in town knows Cletus's uncle is a scoundrel," I answer. "I noticed them talking and—just have my suspicions."

Mrs. Barley doesn't respond immediately, but seems to be trying to focus on the direction of my voice before saying, "Harold, I may be blind, but that doesn't mean I can't see some things. Let me handle Cletus. I've been doing that most of his life. I believe people get out of life what they put into it. I appreciate your concern, but it's unnecessary."

"I hope you're right," I reply.

"What's you talkin' about?" Cletus asks, as he nervously stumbles back into the room carrying a glass of tea.

"Not anything to concern you," Mrs. Barley replies, before I can answer.

"I guess I better get home," I say, after taking a sip of the sweet tea.

"Don't be a stranger, Harold," Mrs. Barley says. "And thanks for bringing out that spray. It was helpful."

I nod and show myself out the door. Once outside, I take one last look at the rundown farm before driving away.

Two months passed before Mrs. Barley's obituary showed up in the newspaper. I attended her service along with many others at the First Christian Church on a Saturday morning. It was a fitting service for a nice woman. Mrs. Barley had only one surviving relative, a nephew who was a banker or some kind of businessman from Chickasha. I would miss having the Barleys for customers, but later that afternoon, I returned to the business of running the store and living my life.

It was a few months after Mrs. Barley passed away when I next saw Cletus Callaway. The weather had turned brisk, and he shivered for a moment before warming himself in front of the Dearborn heater at the front of my store. I had not kept up with what Mrs. Barley's death had meant to Cletus, but heard rumors he was still living on the farm. Cletus looks different to me in some way, but I have a hard time determining why. He had always been a happy-go-lucky man, but today he has a serious look of concern, of which I'm not accustomed to seeing in him.

"What can I do you for, Cletus?" I greet.

Cletus answers, "I need a pound of roofing nails, and do you have a square of shingles in stock?"

"The plain ones," I reply. "You doing some roofing in this weather?"

"I got to patch a roof," Cletus frowns.

"Where are you living at?" I ask.

"The Barley's old house," Cletus shares. "I—well, old lady Barley left me the house and forty acres in her will."

"She did?"

Cletus nods, "She only had the one nephew, and I guess after all the years I lived on the place she kind of thought of me as kin, too. The nephew over at Chickasha inherited all the money and most of the land, but she left me the house and the forty acres around it."

As I sack up Cletus's nails and scavenge the back isle for packages of shingles, I comment, "I guess that worked out well. You can sell the place to your uncle like you planned."

"No chance of that," Cletus fumes. "Don't know exactly where Cecil is, but he may well be in prison."

"What happened?"

"He ran into some trouble with his investors," Cletus replies. "Something about paying the old investors off with new investors' money. I don't know the details except the Comanche County Sheriff came looking for him and said some people were ready to hang him. I hadn't heard from Uncle Cecil, but the sheriff thought he might have skedaddled into Texas."

"That sounds like Cecil," I say. "So, you finally decided to do some work on the Barley's place? Too bad you didn't do your job when Mrs. Barley was alive."

"You're telling me," Cletus mutters. "The place ain't worth selling, and the bank won't loan on it in the condition it's in. I tried to sell it, but it was no use. The roof's leaking right over my bed, and the wall in the back's in bad shape too. Mrs. Barley's fixed me good."

"What do you mean by that?" I scold. "Seems to me it was a right decent thing she did leaving you a place to stay."

Cletus nods, "She was always on me to do my chores and always sayin' I'd be sorry for not keeping up with things. I let the place go down when she'd been happy to pay for repairs. How was I to know she planned on leaving me the place? If you want my opinion, she's had this plan all along just to teach me a lesson."

"I hate to ask, Cletus, but how will you pay for these nails and shingles? Mrs. Barley's gone—I need to know I'll get paid."

"You don't have to worry about that," Cletus claims. "The old lady fixed that for me too. She left a little money—kind of an allowance with her nephew for me to use on the place. There's no money for me, but I can send the bills for materials to him, and he'll pay up to twenty dollars a month. That's not enough to hire anyone that could get the place in condition to sell, but sure seems enough to keep me busy."

"So, you're still working the farm?" I ask.

Cletus nods, "I have to. It's the only place I can afford to live. I got to patch the roof, and then try to grow some watermelons next summer. Of course, I'll have to dig the old tractor out from under the barn that collapsed and get it running to plow the field."

"You'll have to mend that south fence, too," I offer.

"Don't remind me," Cletus frowns. "There's too much to do and not enough hours in the day. If I patch the roof, at least I'll have a dry place to sleep. It's not too bad, though. The nephew pays the electric so I have the radio in the evenings. Old lady Barley fixed me up pretty good."

"Sounds like she fixed you up fine," I smile.

Cletus looks out at the cold, gray afternoon that is quickly slipping away as he says, "I better get to that roof. With my luck, it'll rain before morning."

"I suspect you better," I reply.

I help Cletus load up his old farm truck and watch him drive unenthusiastically to his evening's work. As his taillights disappear in the distance, I think to myself, Cletus Callaway sure loved his schemes. I guess Mrs. Barley liked hers, too.

THE END

A Confusing End

What kind of place is this? The drab green cinder block walls seem like some kind of prison. An unsmiling man looking meanly at me guards the locked exit. Where am I?

Who are these people? They all seem to be watching me. I don't like the older man. He's always asking me to do things I don't understand. He has an uncomfortable familiarity I don't like. He asks me questions I don't want to answer or asks about people in which he should have no interest.

It's best to keep quiet—keep to myself. I pretend to be pleasant and do my best to keep my thoughts to myself. Who knows what these people want? Who knows what they will use against me in this prison? I stare blankly at the wall, trying desperately to make myself invisible to these people. What do they want, anyway? This is exhausting. Even these strangers seem tired of being here. I want to escape.

My mind wonders to a happier, more adventuresome time. My thoughts are my only diversion. I think back to my school days at a place we called Fuss Box. The school's real name was Martel, but a particularly neurotic teacher, named Mrs. Packard, shouted one day that her classroom was, "nothing more than a Fuss Box." The name stuck.

Frog day is what drove Mrs. Packard to make such a claim. She had an irrational fear of anything reptilian. The boys in the school discovered this on the day we dissected frogs as part of the lesson, and Mrs. Packard turned pale and nearly fainted. The next week, all the boys, and even some of the girls, brought frogs to school and turned them loose in Mrs. Packard's classroom. Mrs. Packard left at the end of the term, but the frogs stayed around the Fuss Box until I left eighth grade.

I can remember Fuss Box like it was yesterday. My younger sister was there. We fought like brothers and sisters will do, but Elizabeth always watched out for me, and she even brought a frog to school that day. Isabel is there as well. She's a friend of Elizabeth, but I see her in a very different way. Her silky brown hair frolics in the breeze. I know this is a memory, but it seems more real than anything else in my life does. This is the day I realize Isabel was a girl, and I was a boy that could tell the difference. Everything is real. The smells, the feelings, the people, all the memories of my youth are there—and they are mine.

"Where's Isabel," I mutter almost to myself. I'm back from my dream, and these strangers are still here. I don't understand. "Where's Isabel!" I repeat. "Where's Elizabeth!"

I realize I've said too much and attracted the attention of the older man. He scowls and starts walking toward me. I know what's to come. He'll use that patronizing tone and try to convince me I'm out of my mind. I brace for his scolding, but he stops a few steps from me and motions to a young man standing at the other end of the room.

"Bobby!" I hear the man say forcefully. "Come see to your grandfather."

I watch the young man walk toward me with an uncomfortable smile. He looks familiar, but not completely. I should know him, but can't make the connection. It will be okay. I'll figure it all out.

"How are you feeling today, Grandpa?" the young man greets.

Grandpa? I think to myself. He's talking to me. He thinks I'm his grandfather. Could it be? The boy looks familiar. He looks like someone I once knew.

"I'm fine," I respond to this boy that I should know.

"Do you know me?" he asks, with a slight look of concern.

"Yes," I reply. "Bobby."

The young man smiles, "That's right, I'm Bobby. It's been a few weeks since I've visited. Looks like they have quite a party planned for you today."

Bobby? That's familiar. I know a Bobby. My son had a boy named Bobby, but he's just a boy. This is a young man and can't be Bobby, but maybe he is. I get confused. I look around the crowded room and notice some decorations and a cake. Is it my birthday? How could that be? Why are these strangers here? What do they want?

"We're having a party," I proclaim.

Bobby smiles, "I know. We're here for your party."

"Yes," I manage to mutter.

"You've had a few of these, haven't you?" Bobby states, trying hard to make conversation.

"I suppose I have," I reply.

"What was your favorite?" Bobby asks.

"I don't know," I answer. After hesitating a moment, I say, "I remember Mama would always make a cake for our birthdays. Sometimes she would bring it to the school. Old Mrs. Packard called the place a Fuss Box, and the name stuck. I remember that she hated frogs so all of us boys made a plan to bring as many frogs as we could catch to school one day. We waited until Mrs. Packard started class and then let the frogs loose. Most of the girls screamed, and Mrs. Packard decided that day she had had enough of teaching and resigned at the end of the year."

"What happened to her?" Bobby asks.

I'm not prepared for the question, but I'm always eager to talk about the old days as I reply, "I don't know that anyone knew. She left town and probably got married. Fuss Box was a rowdy school, and we rarely had a teacher for more than a year back then. I'll have to check up on her and find out where she went. People will want to know."

"What year was that?" Bobby asks. "What years were you at Fuss Box?"

I'm able to give Bobby the answer to his question without hesitation, but I'm now worried he'll ask more questions which I cannot answer. I know full well the year I finished eighth grade, but I'm much more confused as to what year this is or how old I am now.

"Where's Isabel?" I ask. I partly want to know where Isabel is, but mainly want to keep this young man from asking more questions that I don't want to answer.

Bobby looks strangely at me. He scans the room as if looking for someone that I don't see.

"Grandma passed on two years ago," Bobby says, in almost a whisper. "Don't you remember?"

"Yes," I lie. "Of course."

Isabel can't be gone; I think to myself. Isabel's my wife. We met in the eighth grade. She was friends with my sister. She's too young to be gone. I'm so confused, but I think Bobby must be mistaken.

"I need to go see Aunt Patty," Bobby says, as he reaches down to touch my hand.

I nod, somewhat relieved to have him go. As he walks away, I try to reconcile that he could be my grandson. How old am I? I look down at my weathered hands, and nothing seems real. Can I be this old man? Whose birthday is this? Where is Isabel?

The older man walks closer. I look away and try to retreat to my memories.

"How are you doing, Dad," the old man greets, with a tone of resignation and duty.

"Fine," I curtly inform. "I want to go home."

The man looks strangely at me as he says, "Dad, this is your home now. Don't you remember us talking about this—just yesterday? You need more help than we can give you at home."

"Take me home," I demand. "I want to go now!"

The man sighs heavily as he says, "We'll get you to bed in a little while, but look at all these people who have come to see you."

I see the people, but don't know what they're doing here.

"Where's Isabel?" I ask.

"Dad," the man sighs. "Mom's not with us anymore. She passed away. Don't you remember?"

I nod, but nothing makes sense. I don't know these people. I want to see Isabel. I want to go home. The man seems content that I nodded. He doesn't want me to make a scene. I let my mind slip back to a better time.

I can remember Fuss Box like it was yesterday. My younger sister is there. We fought like brothers and sisters will do, but Elizabeth always watched out for me, and she even brought a frog to school that day. Isabel is there, as well. She's a friend of Elizabeth, but I see her in a very different way. Her silky brown hair frolics in the breeze.

The older man has stepped away and is leaving me alone, for now. He talks to another man. They think I can't hear them, but I can make out most of their conversation.

"How is he?" the man says.

"About the same."

"I had no idea."

"He was able to keep it hidden for a long time. If you weren't around him that much, he seemed to be functioning pretty well. He could make conversation, talk about the weather. He liked to talk about the old times and that seemed to be what he could fall back on. As things got worse, he repeated himself. All the old stories were like a tape recording that got played back over and over. The tape's getting shorter all the time, and he's having a hard time remembering even the family. I'm not sure he even recognizes Bobby anymore, but who knows. Who knows if he even knows who I am anymore?"

"I hated to hear about your mother," the other man says. "She was a fine woman."

"It was hard at the end. She kept her mind, but her heart just gave way. The last few years were difficult for her. I wish we had taken him to a care facility earlier. She worried about him, but I don't think he would have known. It would have given her some rest."

Who are they talking about? I think to myself. How could they be so uncaring to this poor fellow? I hope I'm never a burden. I don't want people talking about me the way they have. I hope I die before I get old. I don't want to think about it. I don't want to have to deal with that man anymore. I want to retreat to my memories. They are always mine.

I can remember Fuss Box like it was yesterday. My younger sister is there. We fought like brothers and sister will do, but Elizabeth always watched out for me, and she even brought a frog to school that day. Isabel is there, as well. She's a friend of Elizabeth, but I see her in a very different way. Her silky brown hair frolics in the breeze. I know this is a memory, but it seems more real than anything else in my life. This is the day I realize Isabel was a girl, and I was a boy that could tell the difference. Everything is real. The smells, the feelings, the people, all the memories of my youth are there—and they are mine.

"I'm about to leave, Grandpa," the young man Bobby interrupts. "You've had quite a day. Thanks for the stories."

"Have I told you about Fuss Box?" I ask.

Bobby smirks, "A few times."

"I remember the day we brought all the frogs to Mrs. Packard's class," I continue. "You see she hated any kind of snake or reptile. She nearly fainted the day we dissected the frogs so we all decided to bring a frog to school the next day. The girls screamed, although my sister Elizabeth was never afraid of frogs. She was best friends with Isabel. Those were good days. I thought old Mrs. Packard was going to run out of the schoolhouse when those frogs started hopping around. We had a lot of fun at Fuss Box."

"Sounds like you were always up to something," Bobby says. "I've got to go. It was good to see you again."

"Good to see you," I reply. "Come again, and I'll tell you about the time we brought the frogs to Mrs. Packard's class."

"I will," Bobby smiles, as he walks away.

He's a nice young man. I'm not sure who he is, but he liked to listen to my stories. There must be some kind of party going on. I look around and nothing seems familiar. Everything seems confusing. What kind of place is this? The drab green cinder block walls seem like some kind of prison. An unsmiling man looking meanly at me guards the locked exit. Where am I?

THE END

THE FATHER ROAD

My father was a rational, responsible, and reasonably sensible man fifty-one weeks out of the year. His calm wisdom, patient understanding, and levelheadedness, however, abandoned him during our annual summer vacation. It was not a matter of him liking vacations; the problem was he liked them too much. He always wanted to get the most out of our family fun time in ways that created stress for even my kindhearted mother.

Dad had a few quirks, I learned to appreciate them later in life, which seemed to manifest themselves during vacation. Anything that looked fun or cost money was immediately branded a "tourist trap" and was thus avoided like leprosy. Almost any attraction, outside of national parks, monuments, and sometimes state parks, were off limits. The more signs and advertisements used on the highway to attract interest or motivate one of us to say, "That looks fun," increased Dad's resolve to avoid the clever marketing. My two brothers and I would then receive the requisite lecture on the value of a dollar…and sometimes a quarter. Succumbing to advertising tricks was a sign of weakness of character to Dad.

Restaurants were closely akin to tourist traps. Why would anyone pay someone to bring us food when Mom was perfectly capable of buying sandwich essentials at the supermarket and "whipping up something to eat" on a moment's notice? Mom's joy of vacationing was getting to wait on us hand and foot—like most other days at our house. Equal to his aversion to restaurants was Dad's distaste at the idea of renting a motel room. Sometimes he would relent for a cabin at a state park, but a typical highway motel was too much of a tourist trap, had too many fun amenities like a swimming pool, and cost money. Real families camped in tents on vacation, and we were a real family.

In the late 1960s, my dad classified all undesirable people into one of three categories: hippies, hobos, and teenagers. Any boy with hair touching his ears was obviously a hippie. Likewise, any girl not wearing a dress was also suspicious to him as possibly being a hippie or leaning toward being a hippie. Hobos did not have to have long hair, but Dad classified anyone that did not seem to have a regular job requiring a shirt, tie, or a name badge to be in this category.

The group Dad most despised was the teenager. He had a certain tone of voice he used in saying the word "teenager" that demonstrated his distrust and angst at this type of human being. Someone broke a window; it must have been teenagers. Someone screeches the tires; it must have been teenagers. Any crime, any vandalism, or any mischief had to be teenagers. I would be a teenager in three years myself and greatly feared I would be asked to leave the house at that point.

Our family's goal on summer vacation was to cover as many miles as possible per day. I listened to a planning session Dad had with my uncle and heard him say, "There's no reason we can't cover 750 miles a day." That's true, if you don't mind driving deep into the night, never bothering to stop and see anything. Who was I to question Dad, however? He was wise, experienced, and possessed the leadership qualities requisite with being Dad. Everything made sense to me, because he was Dad. Besides, there wasn't much to see, since "tourist traps" covered so much of the western United States.

Mention the Grand Canyon and Dad believed it might be an optical illusion. Yellowstone, "the government pumps all that water through the pipes to make the geysers, just so they can charge people five dollars to see Old Faithful." To Dad, the Interstate Highway System was the eighth wonder of the world and the best thing to come out of World War II. You could see anything through the window of the car at 70 miles per hour.

Mom hoped traveling with her sister's family would perhaps soften Dad and make the vacation more relaxing. I wondered who she thinks she's been living with the past twelve years. My Uncle Roy was much like my dad, just not as sophisticated. Roy had never been out of the state, but was eager to match Dad's enthusiasm for seeing as much of the southwestern United States in one week as possible. Their plan was simple: cross the Mississippi River in the early morning hours, trek across the Midwest, and eventually see the Grand Canyon. It was only 1,528 miles. A good two days' drive there, one day to see the canyon, and three days back to see the rest of the sights in the great Southwest.

My "vacation" started before dawn...really the middle of the night. My mother gently nudged my brothers and me awake before whispering that we could continue our sleep in the station wagon. We drove across town to meet up with my aunt, uncle, and their two daughters. My female cousins were older...teenagers, and looked none too happy to be forced into the family car to follow us across country. Dad became impatient at having to wait for Uncle Roy to have his morning cup of coffee. After a few mutterings of already being behind schedule, Dad accelerated the station wagon aggressively, and we headed out of town on US Highway 60.

I slept comfortably in the back of the station wagon until Dad excitedly reported, "There's the mighty Mississippi, boys!" I rubbed my eyes to see the dark waters of the great river near Cairo, Illinois, where the Mississippi, and Ohio Rivers converge. I'm sure it would have been a marvelous sight, if it hadn't been in the dead of night. I went back to sleep and woke up with the sun about the time we drove through Poplar Bluff, Missouri.

Dad stopped for gas and asked who needed to use the restroom. My brothers and I took any chance to get out of the car and explore the wonders of the Phillip's 66 station. I made the mistake of asking Dad if I could use one of my dimes in the Coca Cola® machine sitting out front. He was not encouraging and explained I would have much better opportunities to spend the $2.57 I had saved from my allowance. Mom had brought a thermos of cherry Kool-Aid, so I took Dad's advice.

My girl cousins had the pitiful look of prisoners. Sandy's fifteen with a prospective boyfriend she left behind, while Debbie was just normally surly to her parents. Debbie, at age twelve, was not a real teenager. She was nice to us, so my brothers and I were naturally drawn to her. Uncle Roy was not as disciplined as my father. His daughters bought Orange Crush® sodas from the pop machine at the gas station. Debbie endeared herself to us even more by giving us a sip. The gas station in Poplar Bluff also became the site of our first "incident" of the trip.

As Dad hurriedly shooed us into the back of the station wagon a "hippie, hobo, teenager" approached to ask, "Hey man, could you spare some change?"

"What?" my father replies, with equal parts indignation, disgust, and amazement.

"My old lady and me are heading to Colorado and need a couple of bucks for gas," the man explains. "I could mail it to you."

Dad stares at the young man a moment before saying, "Get a job." When the man hesitates to retreat, Dad reluctantly hands him two dollars.

For the next twenty miles, we receive a lecture from Dad about the value of work, the ills of laziness, and the unforgivable sin of being a hippie, hobo, or teenager. Outside of Springfield, Missouri, enticing signs for Fantastic Caverns and Marvel Cave cause my mother to meekly state, "A cave tour might be educational for the boys."

Without hesitation Dad replies, "A tourist trap—and we don't have time."

We ride silently through the remainder of Missouri. The Oklahoma border creates our second "incident" on the trip. Soon the "incidents" became too numerous to count. Dad rolls into Oklahoma on the Interstate Highway system in a relatively relaxed demeanor until a most disgusting four-letter word shows up on a sign, "Toll."

Dad's plan did not include a toll road. A toll road costs money. A toll road was the ultimate tourist trap. We are served an hour-long sermon on the evils of Oklahoma and how unthinkable it was to charge someone to drive on a public road. It was unfair. It was un-American. The toll road was barely tolerable to him, but when we stop at the first gate to pay, he got his revenge by lecturing the tollgate attendant about the evils of swindling un-expecting tourists with a "taxation without representation." My mother, always the diplomat, asked about the signs that said, "Don't Drive Into Smoke." The tollgate attendant dryly stated the Indians were on the warpath, again. My brothers and I were intrigued, but Dad was not. He drove off determined not to spend a dime in Oklahoma.

At his first opportunity, Dad ditched the toll road and decided to drive the old Route 66 highway slicing through eastern Oklahoma. It was fine with my brothers and me, as we experienced some of the small towns invisible from the interstate. The detour was costing Dad precious time, however, and testing his patience at having to drive through the small towns. By the time we spent two hours navigating Tulsa, Dad swallowed his pride and paid to drive the toll road. We buzzed through Oklahoma City and fortunately found the interstate turned back to a free road. The terrain became flatter and barer, and Dad was now making good time on a free road. We stopped in Clinton, Oklahoma for gas. Dad had sworn to not spend a penny in the state that sponsored toll roads, but Uncle Roy passed us and insisted on stopping. It was getting late. We managed a roadside picnic at the gas station in what must have been the windiest place on earth. After wrestling paper plates and spilling the red Kool-Aid on my blue jeans, we were back on the road.

We witnessed a magnificent sunset as we exited Oklahoma. Dad was glad to be out of the state and now looked for a place to camp near Shamrock, Texas. As best I can remember, there was not a park or anything resembling a tree in west Texas. I believed it to be the flattest place on earth. Dad pulled into a rest stop. Since there was no sign forbidding camping, we pitched our tents as Dad and Uncle Roy battled the wind sweeping across the Great Plains.

Sandy and Debbie were quick to note that although the rest area had a bathroom that closed at ten o'clock, there were no showers. My brothers and I saw this as a good thing, but the girls seemed to think this primitive. My dad and Uncle Roy were satisfied with their camp, but my mother and aunt quickly huddled at a nearby picnic table. In a few minutes, the women came to complain about the facilities and location so near the interstate highway. Dad had a look of disbelief that there was anything with which to be concerned. The campsite was free, and better yet near the road, so that we would waste no time in the morning getting back on the road. Mother restated her concerns, and Dad conceded that tomorrow night they would find a more suitable camp area—even if they had to pay a fee.

Dad lit the Coleman stove, and Mom dutifully cooked chicken fried steak for our supper. It was past dark by the time dinner was ready. My brothers and I were permitted to eat our meat and corn on the cob with our fingers. After a trip to clean up in the rest area's restroom, we had completed our first day of vacation.

I learned on that trip that the summer days in west Texas were very hot, but the nights could be cool to almost cold. It was before sunrise when Mom nudged us awake again to start making miles toward our destination. Once the car warmed up, I slept soundly in the back of the station wagon wedged between the cooler and two giant suitcases. I did not see more of Texas and woke up somewhere in New Mexico when it was time for more fuel. As we pass Tucumcari, New Mexico, Mom comments about the number of interesting motels. Dad reminds her we have a tent.

Mom held her tongue through Tucumcari and Albuquerque, but by the time we reached the Arizona border, she'd had enough driving. It was late afternoon as we approached the Petrified Forest National Park. The very name sounded like a tourist trap to Dad. He initially resisted, but he could tell Mom had made up her mind. It was a national park, after all. The park was near the interstate, and the Visitor's Center was free. Dad had no other arguments, although I'm sure I heard him mutter that we might not make the full 750 miles today.

The Petrified Forest National Park was a nice break, but somewhat disappointing to my brothers. It looked like much of the desert we had watched go by the station wagon's window for the day, except with rocks looking like tree trunks. Dad's initial reluctance to stop vanished when he realized this attraction cost no money. He proceeded to take over as tour guide, and for the next forty minutes, we were educated on the history of the strange rocks and the wonders of nature.

More interesting to us was the gift shop in the Visitor's Center stocked with polished rocks, Indian-looking souvenirs fresh from Japan, vanity miniature license plates with our names, and even "Mexican jumping beans." My brothers and I wanted to sample all of the goods, but Dad gently reminded us that we had a long vacation, and we would be wise to save our money until the trip back. Sandy and Debbie had no such restrictions and left the gift shop with a key chain and one of those license plates with their names handsomely displayed.

By the time we finished the Petrified Forest National Park, Dad was hopelessly behind schedule and had no chance of making it to the Grand Canyon that day. Uncle Roy became our new hero when he suggested we stop at one of those McDonald's for a hamburger, fries, and shake. My brothers and I were ecstatic at the prospect. Dad instinctively refused, but after a stern look from my mother, he agreed. Later he even consented to paying five dollars to stay at a KOA campground that had a pool and showers. Of course, we arrived after dark and could not use the pool, but Mom made sure we all were thoroughly rinsed in the communal shower. After paying for supper and a campsite, I'm pretty sure I heard Dad weeping in his corner of the tent that night.

We arrived at the Grand Canyon a day late but well worth the wait. It was simply a canyon that could only be described as grand. My brothers and I ran up to every rail to lean over the abyss as Mom frantically shouted for Dad to get a hold of us. Unfortunately, there were three of us, and he only had two arms. Mother was nearly hysterical all day. Dad uncharacteristically let us do something fun and allowed me to walk down into the canyon with Debbie and Sandy. We made it almost four hundred yards before I became dehydrated and fainted. Dad got to carry me out of the canyon. That was pretty much the end of the Grand Canyon experience for me.

The rest of our trip to Arizona went pretty much to plan—that is nothing really worked out well. We took a detour to the Hoover Dam. A tour guide entertained us by explaining we were on the "Dam Tour." My mother blushed, but my brothers and I were greatly amused at the profane sounding attraction. Dad told us the dam was named after Herbert Hoover, a greatly misunderstood president. Dad went on to explain Republicans were basically good, decent folks that respected law and order. Democrats mostly catered to hippies and teenagers and were not be trusted. All in all, we had a good time and greatly enjoyed our adventure to Arizona.

We made our way around to the north rim of the Grand Canyon, coming dangerously close to the ultimate tourist trap—Las Vegas. Uncle Roy really wanted to take a side trip to Vegas, but Dad was resolute and determined to keep his family away from anything that might look fun or cost money. By the time the week was over, Uncle Roy was homesick and ready to end this odyssey. I overheard Uncle Roy asking Dad if he thought we might be home by Sunday. Dad put his arm around him and explained if we drove real hard for two days, we might—might make it home. I thought my uncle would cry. Dad, always sensitive to the needs of others, assured Uncle Roy he had a plan that would take us home a different route avoiding Oklahoma's senseless toll roads. It would add a little time to our trip back, but we would see new country and save almost a buck fifty in tolls. My uncle groaned in utter resignation, and our party headed east.

My brothers and I swarmed the last souvenir shop in Arizona. Dad ran out of excuses for us to save our allowance, and we finally purchased life-long treasures to commemorate our epic vacation. A dollar and quarter bought me a miniature license plate with my name. My middle brother, Doug, wasted his money on some polished rocks. My little brother, Stevie, was also "gypped' when he bought Mexican jumping beans in a plastic box. The beans, according to the label, would jump, pop, and practically dance a jig. They looked as useless as the polished rocks to me, and rested helplessly in a small plastic box. We were satisfied with our souvenirs and ready for home.

Dad acquired a massive map from the Phillips 66 Company showing the entirety of the western United States to plan this trip. The map almost covered the front windshield when fully unfurled. To Dad, the map was his navigational Bible, which he cherished because it gave him knowledge and power. As best I remember, my mother never folded it once to his satisfaction.

Dad's plan for the return trip included an educational adventure in a place on the map he circled called Four Corners— the only place in the United States where four states met at one point. Dad was extremely excited. We could see four states at one time, and the place was free. After living in tents for most of a week, Uncle Roy and Dad decided it would be a good night to sleep under the desert stars at Four Corners. The boys would use our sleeping bags outside, and the girls could sleep in the station wagon and across the car seats. The tents would stay packed and save us valuable time the next morning.

I'm not sure what the annual rainfall is at Four Corners, but I've never seen so much water come down for so hard as I did on the evening we pulled up to the large slab of stone marking the four corners of the states. Uncle Roy tried to pitch his tent, but a gust of wind sent his canvas tumbling across the gravel parking lot. He had to throw the wet mess into his trunk. What happened next was the longest night of my life as we tried to sleep in the two vehicles sitting upright. My brother tried to strangle me with the seatbelt. Mother did not say a word, but even a preteen like me could feel the tension.

As is always the case, things looked brighter in the light of day. Four Corners was a vacant piece of desert except for a large paved square marking the borders of Utah, Arizona, Colorado, and New Mexico. I did not realize how stale the inside of our station wagon was until I breathed the rain-freshened desert air. It was Sunday, and that meant church for our family. The closest town with a church of our choosing was Cortez, Colorado.

Mother was almost frantic. Dad suggested that maybe we could skip church just this once. Mother did not answer him, but her stern stare telegraphed that we would be attending church this Sunday. Uncle Roy and his family agreed to go with us, but after a night in the car we were a mess. Mother endured a lot during this week but going to church looking less than our best was too much for her.

"We need to check into a motel," Mother proposed.

My dad started his well-rehearsed refusal, but before he could get out two words Mother says, "That wasn't a suggestion! Check into a motel!"

My father proudly wore the pants in our family, but only when Mother let him. His argument was over. My mild-mannered mother had spoken. He was going to rent a motel, if only for an hour.

In retrospect, I would have liked to see my dad ask for the "hourly room rate." I'm confident the motel Dad chose had rented rooms by the hour routinely, but probably not on a Sunday morning for a family to prepare for church. Dad secured keys to a single room, and soon Mother orchestrated a steady line of people taking a quick shower and putting on the best clothes they had left. Mother had packed church clothes for us. Dad even managed to save back one clean shirt, although Mother was not happy he didn't bring a tie. My cousins and aunt also made themselves presentable. Uncle Roy, however, did not fare as well.

Uncle Roy came out of the shower with a white towel wrapped around him. The room was crowded, but everyone took a step back when he appeared. To this day, I've never seen a man with more hair on his body. His thick sideburns should have been an indication that his back and chest would resemble a bear or gorilla as much as a man. Uncle Roy was not embarrassed to stand in the room wearing only a towel, but something else bothered him.

"I need a shirt," Uncle Roy proclaimed. "I've been wearing the one I changed out of for two days and slept in it to boot."

My dad looked at my mother sheepishly before saying, "I don't have anything left except this shirt I wore yesterday."

Uncle Roy smiled, "I'll take it! It beats anything I have left."

My aunt looked as if she might faint, and my cousins appeared equally humiliated. In a few more minutes, Uncle Roy was dressed wearing Dad's used shirt, and we were out of the motel in less than an hour.

The church in Cortez was located close to the highway. I'm sure they had seen their fair share of people down on their luck. The old preachers would say, "Every skunk has its pew." I can't imagine what we looked—or smelled like, but let's just say the people in Cortez were less than friendly when we settled into the comfortable, padded pew. A kindly older man approached to introduce himself and ask, "If we needed anything." Mother quickly assured him we were fine and just on vacation. The old man smiled as if he understood.

Although Mother insisted we needed church, I can honestly say I remember little of the sermon, song service, or prayer. I do remember how comfortable the pews were and how good air conditioning felt for the first time in a week. Before the first prayer, I was enjoying a restful, deep sleep. I think I could have slept the whole service, and I think my mother would have understood. Fate had different plans.

During communion, when the entire congregation entered the quietest point in the service, a faint sound awakened me. At home, my mother would have shaken me awake, but this was an entirely different distraction. It started with a sound that I had never heard. In the quiet of the church, a distinctive and repetitive popping sound echoed through the silence. My mother gave me a stern look, but I shrugged in an attempt to prove my innocence. The sound became stronger and more noticeable as now both my parents desperately searched for the source coming unmistakably from our pew. The service was nearing an end, when Mother was able to isolate the now loud clicking sound coming from my brother's pocket. Mother snapped her fingers, which caused even more of a ruckus, to instruct my brother to empty his pockets. I can still remember the joy on his face and the horror on my mother's, as what he had thought were "dud" Mexican jumping beans, came vivaciously to life during communion.

Jumping beans have some kind of moth inside the seedpod causing it to jump. No doubt, the combination of warmth of his thigh where the beans were pressed, along with the possible agitation of him peeing his pants, which he was prone to do at the time, brought the moths to a state of excitement. Mother grabbed the small plastic box that stored the magical beans and shook them vigorously, as if that might help. It might have had the box not flown open, scattering the beans across several rows of pews.

My brother, now fully awake, scampered underneath the pews before Mother could grab him to retrieve his prize. Communion continued somehow, but I remember snickers from the congregation. None of the laughter came from my mother, however. As soon as the final "Amen" was said, she was making apologizes to as many as she could in the congregation, although I was sure we would never see any of them again. I'm quite positive the people in Cortez were happy and relieved to see Dad drag us out the doors of the church to continue our vacation.

Somewhere around La Junta, Colorado, Dad stopped for gasoline. He and Uncle Roy carefully calculated the number of hours it would take to drive straight through to end the agony of this vacation. After the church incident, Mother seemed nearly comatose to anything around her. Dad suggested a trip through Dodge City might be interesting. Uncle Roy agreed, but only if we kept moving.

As Dad wrangled us back into the station wagon for the retreat home, we looked like vagabonds. A familiar face approached Dad—the longhaired "hippie," who asked for help at our first stop in Poplar Bluff. Dad listens more than talks, and the longhaired man hands him something before walking away. Dad returns to the car with the look of a beaten man.

"What did he want?" Mother asks.

Dad starts the car without responding.

"Well, what did he want?" Mother repeats.

Dad frowns, "He gave me back the two dollars I gave him in Poplar Bluff."

"What?" Mother shrieks.

Dad shrugs, "He said, 'Man you look like you could use this more than me. Stay cool.'"

"What did you do?" Mother quizzes.

"I took the two dollars back," Dad defiantly says. "I wish I'd found him earlier. We could have taken the short way back through Oklahoma."

THE END

THE LETTER

March 10, 1862

Dear Parents, Sisters, & Brothers:

We desire to let you know we are well and the brittle thread of life has not severed as yet. The kind hand of providence has restored, and is preserving our health and is giving us a sufficiency of daily bread to maintain life, and I hope that God our Heavenly Father, and great benefactor is breaking sufficiently of the bread of eternal life with our never perishing soul daily and hourly.

Mr. John Love has been in Camp three or four days, and intends to start home in the morning. By him I expect to send this letter. It is the Holy Sabbath eve, and we are stationed for a few days at most, after marching part of the morning. We have stopped near Van Buren, to have horses shod.

Doubtless you are aware our army is marching Eastward, I suppose, from what I have heard, that the front is in Pope, by this time. I regret to the very depths of my soul that we are compelled to leave this section of our much beloved land exposed to our cruel enemies. I cannot believe we are giving it up on account of our foes, but on the account of the scarcity of subsistence.

Major Brodis' Battalion is the rear guard. Most of the boys are in good health now. When we get our horses shod we will be in fine plight for service again. It is a lamentable thing that our army had to stay in this section of the country so long. They have consumed nearly everything for man and beast, from Van Buren northward to the line is one continued scene of desolation and ruin.

There is nothing to cheer the desponding heart of man, I mean every true Southern man. We face a formidable force, a terrible army of mercenary wretches, of black republican myrmidons, and northern vandals who invade our once smiling, happy land that freedom called her own, and is spreading ruin and desolation wherever it goes. Dark forebodings are seen at every step. Bright hopes are being blasted, and every prospect baffled. I hope to see a very agreeable change take place ere long. I have not lost all hopes yet, or trust in God. I place great confidence in the slender thread of prayer that moves the hand of omnipotence. I pray that the strong arm and right hand of God may give us the victory yet.

Like the Psalmist David I pray for the temporal destruction of my enemies. Yet I pray that God may bless their souls, and dispose their hearts to peace, if I err God forgive.

Perhaps this battalion will pass through Pope in a few days. If so, I will apply for permission to come by home. I am not sure that it will be granted, for Major Brooks will not allow some of his men to go home tonight who do not live more than four miles from the camp. He has several under guard for threats to go home anyhow. If I do not get to come home, I will have to leave some of my clothes somewhere. My horse is getting very thin. King Wood's back is very sore. So sore he cannot be rode.

Dear Ma, I expect you are making soap at this time. If you can, please have some caked soap made. We need such and I will take some of it with me to wash my clothes. Pa, if the army has not taken all of your corn, fodder and oats by this time, I will advise you to try to conceal enough in the woods, in some cluster of bushes, and hide it, for I tell you truthfully that the last ear has been taken from some families up here. Though if you have any to spare, let them have it. Let them have every grain you can spare, also every bind of fodder and oats. Several of our wounded are getting in a pinch. Fowler was killed. I must close. I hope you are all well.

Your Sons Affectionately,
R.R. & W.B. Perry

Mabel Perry looked at this letter every day. She learned to be more careful when she once let her tears smudge some of the writing. The letter represented the last contact she had with her boys. Robert had been the more studious of the two. He wished to enter the ministry until the War Between the States called him to duty for the Arkansas Militia as a First Lieutenant. Billy was the more impetuous brother. He had been the one eager to fight the Yankees.

Robert, with Billy looking over his shoulder she assumed, penned the letter March 10, 1862: two days after the Battle at Elk Tavern in Arkansas and a month before the bigger battle at Shiloh in Tennessee. Two years after the war, the letter still haunts her. The boys survived the Battle at Elk Tavern. That opportunity to rid Arkansas of the Yankees invading from Missouri was squandered. Her sons and Cousin Daniel bivouacked in Pope County not more than a three-hour horse ride from home, but they marched east before she could deliver the soap Robert requested. She picked up the few possessions her boys had left behind, but they were gone to Corinth, Mississippi. Arkansas had been abandoned after Elk Tavern, and its army commissioned to stop Grant in Mississippi.

Shiloh had been a great and terrible battle with thousands on both sides slaughtered. She remembered checking those dreadful lists at the post office of the killed, wounded, and missing. She prayed every day her boys' names would not appear, and that prayer was answered—temporarily. A week after Shiloh, she learned the Arkansas regiment arrived after the great battle. She slept well for several nights, believing her boys safe—at least for a few days.

Robert wrote regularly to let her know the condition of himself and his brother, but then the letters stopped. She had not been too concerned, but after a month, her relief at knowing her sons missed the battle at Shiloh turned to dread. She went to town to investigate, but no one knew anything about the boys from Russellville.

The Browns and the Gordons had three sons each in the regiment, but neither family had heard a word. Mabel Perry was not too surprised. The Browns and the Gordons were simple farm folk, and not likely to write many letters. Her concern grew, however, after visiting the Boids, Troys, Gideons, Sunkers, McEvers, Dukes, Burkheads, Berrymans, Erwins, Jacksons, Soves, Foremans, and Millers. None of the families had heard from the men who left Pope County. She passed by the Fowler place on her way home. Timmy Fowler had been the only casualty during the Elk Tavern battle. His death had been an accident since the Russellville boys had not been in direct combat during that battle. Timmy Fowler, probably in his excitement, fell from his horse as the army retreated to the south and east.

The Fowler farm was a sad and pitiful site to her. The land itself was suitable for crops, but Timmy had been the only son. The Fowlers, like almost everyone else in Pope County, owned no slaves and could not afford to hire help, even if there had been an eligible man left in the county. Mr. Fowler had done his best, but the place looked rundown, and he did not seem to have the will to keep working it. Mr. Fowler died the next spring and his wife the winter after that. Now she understands their despair at having lost so much.

Mabel Perry's farm had always been for her boys—for the family. They had worked for a generation to secure a future. Her husband lost his will to live after the boys disappeared and died before knowing the war was lost. She finds herself a widow and all alone on the farm that steadily deteriorates just as the Fowler farm had. Her boys disappeared into the abyss of the war. The worst part to her is not knowing what happened to them on the way to Shiloh. Nobody has answers for her.

Like most in her part of Arkansas, she had been naïve and overly enthusiastic about the war. She had no interest in states' rights, the Missouri Compromise, or the issue of slave states or free. Outsiders were determined to invade their "once smiling, happy land that freedom called her own." She learned to hate the Yankee invaders. She had developed a less than gracious opinion about many of the Confederates, as well. She had tired of hearing about "the cause." All she knew is her boys were gone and nothing could fill that void.

Over the past five years, she had read the letter every day and could quote it without queue. The words, "We face a formidable force, a terrible army of mercenary wretches…northern vandals," seared themselves into her thoughts and attitudes. The war taught her something dark. Her sons' letter prayed for, "the temporal destruction of my enemies. Yet I pray that God may bless their souls, and dispose their hearts to peace, if I err God forgive." After five years of not knowing the fate of her boys, the widow struggled with the reconciliation and forgiveness her son had advocated only days before his disappearance.

A barking dog distracts her, and she realizes she's still holding the letter. Looking out the window, she watches as John Love waddles toward the house. She sighs deeply as she carefully folds her letter and places it securely in the pages of her Bible in the book of Psalms. John was an older gentleman and one of the civic leaders in Russellville. He had been too old for the war, and now finds himself as the protector of many widowed households. He had been a friend to the family for years. John brought the letter to her in March of 1862, when there was still some hope left in the world.

"Come on in, John!" she shouts, before he's twenty steps from the porch.

John Love nods with a forced smile, and after navigating the five steps up the porch, takes a seat.

"It's a nice day," John greets.

She looks around before saying, "Tolerable weather. We got a nice rain last week—almost an inch."

"Yes," John replies. "We got nearly that much at our place."

"What brings you out?" she asks, as she can think of no good reason for John Love to have made a social call on this side of town.

"Nothing particular," he answers, although something in his demeanor causes her to doubt that. "How are things?"

"Look around," she bluntly retorts. "There's no crop in the field this spring and not likely to be one planted. I put out a nice garden, but that's about all I can manage. I paid the mortgage at the end of the year, but I doubt I'll be as lucky next year. There's no men to hire, and even if there was, they would have to work on a promise. I may rent out some of the fields in the fall, if I can find someone that wants to try to rehabilitate them. In short, things are in a mess, but I'm sure you knew that before coming out here."

"I'm afraid so," John sighs.

"So," she says, as she stares sternly at her visitor. "Are you working for the baggers now? Did one of them send you out to see if the place can be picked up for taxes?"

"No," John quickly assures. "I came to see if you have any kin that might be of some help."

"None that are still living," she curtly answers. "Why do you ask?"

John hesitates before explaining, "There's a man new to town asking about you and wanting directions to your place."

"What for?"

"I have no idea," John continues. "I thought you might know. Thought maybe you had some family that could come to your aid."

"None," she assures. "What kind of man? What does he want?"

John shakes his head, "I don't know. He's a—stranger."

"A stranger?"

John nods, "Not from around here."

"Speak your mind, John Love," she demands.

"By the way he talks, he's from up north," John replies. "He's got that fast talking, nasal way they have of speaking."

"A Yankee?" she gasps. "Looking for me?"

"Seems that way," John confirms.

"What's he like?" she inquires.

"Younger fellow," John shares. "Thin as a rail and kind of quiet. Don't look like the kind to find trouble, but he's been asking around town about you. I was hoping it was some kin that had come to help you out, but thought you should know all the same."

"I have no idea," she muses. "What could a Yankee possibly want here?"

John Love looks around before saying, "I think you're about to find out. Here he comes now."

The thin man walks with a slight limp up the pathway toward her house. He has a nervous temperament making it clear he is uncomfortable.

The man walks to the porch steps before asking in his distinctive accent, "Mrs. Perry?"

"Who's asking?" she suspiciously replies.

With a shy nod, the man says, "My name is Daniel Lentz."

She glances at John Love long enough to determine her neighbor does not recognize the name. In as pleasant a voice as she can muster, she says, "What can I do for you—Daniel Lentz?"

"I came about your boy—Robert," Daniel answers. "Wondered if I might have a word sometime?"

"You knew my Robert?" she anxiously quizzes.

"Yes."

"You know what became of him?" she asks, with an unmistakable tone of dread.

The thin man nods.

"Do you need me to stay around, Mabel?" John asks, as he carefully studies the man standing at the foot of the steps.

She hesitates an instant before saying, "No, John. I'll be fine. Why don't you head back to town? I'm interested to know what this Mr. Lentz knows about my boy."

"You're sure?" John asks.

She nods. John stares at the stranger a moment, before shuffling away in his slow gait.

After John has left, she asks, "What happened to my boys?"

The stranger looks down at his worn shoes to say, "I don't know about all your boys, just Robert. He—he might be here now instead of me if things had been different."

She looks at him sternly before managing to offer, "Have a seat. Would you drink some cider? I have some I can bring out."

"That would be nice, ma'am," Daniel Lentz replies, as he nervously moves onto the porch and takes a seat in a cane chair where she motions him to sit.

Mabel Perry disappears into the house with a fountain of emotions tugging at her soul. She has fresh cider stored in the kitchen, but instead of pouring a glass for her visitor, she quietly pulls open the drawer to a bureau in the front room, firmly grasping a loaded pistol. The pistol is heavy and foreboding in her trembling hand. The seeds of her hatred for the Yankees had been sown in reading the letter from her sons. Her hatred grew with the death, the starvation, the humiliation of defeat. The Yankees had taken everything from her, and now one that possibly killed her boy, sits unsuspectingly on her front porch. He's there ready for her judgment with his back to the open window where she had seated him.

The pistol clanks menacingly as she cocks it back to fire. This man, Daniel Lentz, makes a nervous twitch, and she is confident he has heard his fate with the cocked pistol at his back. She expects him to jump up and rush her, or perhaps plead for his life. Instead, he leans forward in his chair as if accepting his fate. The gun shakes violently in her hand. She's sure she can pull the trigger, but somehow cannot. The foolish man stays with his back to her—a perfect target. All she has to do is squeeze.

No one in Russellville would blame her. On the contrary, she's confident people in town would celebrate her revenge. She suspects John Love is organizing a hanging party for this trespasser as she contemplates taking his life—as he had taken her sons away from her. Something keeps her from pulling the trigger. She's not sure how long she has been taking aim, but it seems like minutes, although it is probably mere seconds. For many months, time has not been relevant to her. Slowly she uncocks the pistol and gently puts it back into the drawer from which it came. She dutifully moves to the kitchen, and in a few moments, returns to the porch with her refreshments.

"Thank you," Daniel Lentz says with a lifeless smile, as he grasps the beverage. He takes a sip before saying, "It's very good—just the right amount of sweet and tart."

She studies him carefully as he seems to savor every drop of the cider, as if he has never tasted anything so sweet. He's a pathetic sight and not at all like any of the other Yankees she has encountered since the end of the war. They had all been well fed and cocky with the irritating sense of entitlement that comes with being the victor. This one is different. He's thin as a scarecrow, and seems nervously apologetic.

"Why didn't you shoot?" Daniel Lentz finally asks.

Mabel should be embarrassed for her visitor to know she contemplated taking his life, but she is not. She and this stranger have some connection she cannot yet determine.

She answers him honestly, "I figured a man like you came here for some purpose. I didn't suppose you would have many answers for me if I shot you dead."

He nods and looks down into his now half-empty glass of cider.

"What happened to my boys?" Mabel asks bluntly. "Did you kill them?"

The man shakes his head, "Not directly, I didn't. That I'll swear to you, but I am responsible, and that's part of the reason I'm here."

Mabel does not respond, but instead stares blankly at him, as if daring him to tell her the story.

"It was the week after Shiloh," Daniel Lentz begins. "You can tell I'm no Confederate. My unit was saved from the bloodiness of the battle. We were in reserve, but that meant we were charged with a burial detail that seemed as if it might last an eternity."

"You found my boy at Shiloh?" she asks, trying to confirm what she believed had happened to the boys from Russellville.

"No," the man shakes his head in an exaggerated manner, indicating more than a disagreement with her assumption. It's more as if he's trying desperately to get something out of his head—a memory that seems to haunt him. "After a week of handling the dead, I was about half out of my mind. I volunteered for a patrol charged with securing the perimeter of our camp. You have to understand, I'm not a brave man, but at that point, I believed anything would be better than looking at those hideous and pathetic victims of the battle.

"My group got lost in the fog, and then we had to camp away from the main army. The Confederates had skedaddled back to Mississippi—or at least most of them had. I had the night watch, but I must have fallen asleep. When I woke up, I was alone in a strange land and surrounded by a thick spring fog. I guess my sergeant found me asleep at the post and left me to fend for myself. I wanted to call out something fierce, but didn't dare. I didn't have to wait long. Everyone hears about the great battles and their casualties and glories, but there's a multitude of other smaller battles and skirmishes that happen without fanfare or glory—just death and suffering and pain.

"I didn't know which way to turn, but in a few minutes, I heard shouting and gunfire. I figured it had to be my unit. I was afraid of a fight, but more afraid of being shot as a deserter. I ran blindly through the woods and fog until suddenly I heard a single shot ring out from my left. I tried to keep running, but it was no use. I fell to the ground with my rifle landing several feet out of reach.

"Before I could move, a group of Confederates charged out of the fog. I think they were surprised that it was just me. They were as lost as I was, but thought they would be in for a fight. They were from Arkansas. I was hurt pretty bad, and some of the Confederates wanted to finish me off and head for the fight. Lieutenant Perry stepped in, however, and stopped them. He looked at my leg and put a tourniquet above my knee. The others were impatient to get to the fight. He instructed them to scout the area, but he stayed with me.

"Like I said, the fog was so thick you couldn't see ten steps in any direction. The skirmish turned into a battle. Unfortunately for the boys from Arkansas, they meandered way too close to the main Army of Ohio. I tried to tell them that, but they wouldn't believe me. They charged over the hill and into a fight. Not long after, I heard a fearsome volley. I believe they marched into an ambush. The main Confederates were retreating south, but Bedford's Calvary was covering the retreat with frantic attacks that seemed to come from everywhere. A bullet came out of nowhere. I couldn't tell if it was Federal or Confederate, but it struck your son in the stomach. He wasn't killed immediately, but he was hurt worse than me.

"We were both wounded and found ourselves in a shallow hollow in the fog with a cavalry battle raging around us. Neither of us was sure who was friend or foe, and neither of us knew which way to go for help. If your other son was with that group that charged over the hill, I'm sure they were all killed in battle. If they had listened to Robert, they might have gone the other way. They might have missed the fight altogether that day. I was with your wounded son for most of the next night. He was hurt bad, but he continued to check on my leg. He knew he would not survive his wound and scribbled out a letter addressed to you. He made me promise to see that you got it."

"You were with Robert when he died?" Mabel asks softly.

Daniel Lentz nods.

"You have the letter?" she asks.

The man's countenance fails him for a moment and soon he fights back tears as he shakes his head.

"No," he finally snivels. "He gave me the letter, but that was not a good place for anyone, Confederate or Federal, to be. Bedford's men made one more sweep through our area. I had been with Robert for most of a day before he died. When the Confederates found me with one of their dead officers, I thought I was finished. I was captured and moved south with the retreating Confederates into Mississippi. I kept the letter for as long as I could, but things were tough. I traded the paper for some bread. Eventually I was exchanged and found myself back east in the fighting. I have a limp, but your son saved my leg—and probably my life.

"I think of him often. I wonder if his unit hadn't spotted me, if they would have kept marching south and missed that battle in the fog. I went back home but my family—my father and mother had passed on. I was sick for a long time—sick in my soul. War does that to a man. I remembered the promise I had made to Robert and decided I needed to find you. In a funny way, that's given me some purpose."

"What did the letter say?" Mabel asks.

"I remember most of it," Daniel shares. "He didn't want you to worry. Said he knew he was going to a better place. He was frightened, but tried to be confident he would be in the good in the final judgement. He said he had fought the good fight and finished the race. He—he still believed in his cause and believed his side would prevail, but I believe he hated the idea of war."

"Is that all?" Mabel asks.

"I'm afraid that's all I can remember," Daniel Lentz states. "He was a man of character. I could tell that in the way he treated me and how he held himself in those final hours. He talked about missing home. Everything about this place was remembered fondly by him—especially you. He knew he was finished, but his main concern was leaving you behind."

"Did he suffer much?" Mabel sobs.

"Not much," Daniel consoles, although Mabel cannot tell if the man is lying to her or not. "He was a strong man in the spirit. He would have kept his suffering from me. I'm sorry for your loss. I saw many men die during that cursed war, but I was not closely affected except by your son. I thought you might find some comfort in knowing his final resting place. He's buried by a peaceful little creek a few miles south of Shiloh. I can't tell you exactly where, but he was buried proper. I even tried to say some words, although words don't come natural to me."

"Why did you come, Mr. Lentz?" Mabel asks. "It would have been safer for you to have stayed away."

Daniel Lentz thinks for a moment before answering, "The battlefield's a lonely and isolated place. The greatest fear for most soldiers is that they'll die alone. There's the fear of pain and the knowledge we won't be living the life we could have lived, but there's some comfort in not being forgotten. If I had been the one killed, I think your son would have let my people know. The least I could do was let his family know what happened. You see, I did this for me more than for him. After all the meanness of war, I wanted to do something decent—make some penance."

"I thought about shooting you when you showed up on this porch," Mabel bluntly informs.

Daniel Lentz nods, "I know. I took a chance, but figured you must be a lot like your son. I only spent a day with Robert, but got a good sense of his character. He hated that we were invading his home, but he seemed able to separate the men from the conflict. I don't think he had malice toward anyone. He might have shot a man in battle, but never in the back. It's easy to hate an idea or the color of a uniform, but hard to hate a man face to face. I'm sorry for your loss. He saved my life and lost his in the process. I owed it to him to let you know what happened. We were enemies, but I think if we met in more peaceable times, we might have been good friends."

"Thank you, Mr. Lentz," Mabel says. "You seem to be a decent man, and you've done a decent thing today. Nothing will bring my boys back, but it is good to know they weren't alone."

"I wish I could have brought Robert's letter to you," Daniel Lentz laments.

Mabel smiles, as she reaches for her worn Bible to slip out the last letter she received and that she has cherished. "I have this letter. In the short time you knew my boy, you repeated the things he held dear. I have this one. He didn't intend for it to be his last, but my boy was always comfortable with who he was. I have this letter, and it is more valuable to me than anything I now own in this world. You see, Mr. Lentz, this letter is my boys' memory. You reminded me of that today. For that, I will thank you."

THE END

THE SANCTUARY

Lisa loved the stale smell of paper and aging book bindings at her local library since she was a small girl. Going to the library was always a treat. The quiet, the serenity, and the regimented order, combined with a sense of curiosity, knowledge, and adventure made the library a special place for her. Anything was possible at the library. The librarian would sometimes have to shush other children, but never Lisa. The library was her sanctuary.

She went to college unsure of her future, but a work-study assignment in the university's library quickly steered her into her future. She learned about the evolving profession. The library was more than just books by the time she started her first job. The library meant information, connectivity, and community programs. As she began her career, she saw the library differently: a warm place in winter and a cool place in summer for the community's less fortunate, homeless or near homeless. It was a place for job searchers, aspiring entrepreneurs, and self-published authors to do research. The library of her childhood had been a serene place where stay-at-home moms took their children for enrichment and culture. Now, she saw more working moms using the library as daycare of last resort. With all the changes, challenges, and community expectations, Lisa still loved the library and her job.

James showed up in July that summer. At eight or nine years old, he was a skinny boy with unkempt hair and a gapped-tooth smile. Lisa always promised herself she would not be one of those stereotypical librarians who constantly shushed every child that dare make an unnecessary noise above a whisper in the hallowed halls of the library. She believed the library's purpose was to serve the community and encourage children to explore their potential. James, however, tested her from the first day.

His first offense had been to hide a book under his raggedy tee shirt. Before Lisa could explain the checkout process, James bolted out the front door, nearly knocking one of her best library patrons to the ground. She chased him out the door, but was wearing heels and never had a chance. Lisa assumed that might be the last time she would see the boy again, but in about a week, he slipped back in wearing the same worn pair of blue jeans and tee shirt with a marginally appropriate saying printed on the back.

Lisa did not overact, but carefully avoided eye contact and slowly positioned herself between the boy and the exit. He panicked and bolted toward the door once he saw what she was doing. She managed to grab him by the arm and gently guide him to the service desk.

"I didn't do nothing!" the boy squirmed, as he eyed a security officer who periodically patrolled the downtown library.

"You didn't do anything," Lisa corrected. "At least not today."

"You can't keep me here!" James argued.

Lisa thought for a moment before saying, "You're right. I want the library to be a place you want to be. It obviously is, since you came back—even after taking that book."

James stared at her guiltily. In his young mind, last week might as well have been a lifetime ago. He obviously figured she would have forgotten the incident. Something in the boy's demeanor affected Lisa, however. There was an innocence behind his apparent insolence. Lisa decided to encourage, not scold.

"Do you know what a library card is?" Lisa asked.

"It's like a credit card," James answered.

"Not exactly," Lisa smiled. "It's a card anyone can have, and it's free. You can use the card to check out books—you can borrow almost any book in the library to take home. Anything you want to know can be found out with that card. Later you bring your book back and check out another one."

"Anyone?" James nervously replied. "Even a kid?"

"Even a kid," Lisa assured. "I would like you to have a card."

"Really?"

"Really," Lisa nodded. "The only thing is, I would like you to bring back the book you took the other day. If you don't bring it back, no one else will have the chance to read it. I'll tell you what. I'll do the paper work to get your card, and you bring the book back next time you come. Deal?"

"Deal."

Lisa sent the application home for his parents. James returned the next day with the book he had swiped. She smirked almost uncontrollably when she noticed he obviously forged his mother's signature. Lisa handed him a new library card anyway. The boy stared at the card for a long time, almost as if he could not believe someone had given him anything. He smiled at Lisa and carefully placed the card into the pocket of his worn jeans. From that day on, James typically showed up a few minutes after the library opened and stayed for much of the day.

Lisa grew up with three brothers, two older and one younger and felt she understood how ornery and mischievous boys could be. She caught herself several times those first few days shushing more than she ever thought she would in trying to control the restless and energetic boy. She couldn't ban a young boy from the public library, she thought to herself. Especially after giving him the library card for which he was so proud. There had to be a better way. After taking a deep breath, Lisa realized the boy did not intend to be disruptive, he just had too much energy. She developed a new strategy, which involved bending a few library rules.

"James!" Lisa greeted enthusiastically the next morning when he showed up at her front door.

"Yeah," the boy cautiously and nervously answered.

Lisa assumed the boy was accustomed to the watchful eye of adults. She tried to keep herself from smirking at the boy, who had all of the symptoms of guilt. He may not have known exactly what the librarian had caught him doing, but he was sure the list of complaints was large.

"I notice you spend a lot of time here," Lisa continued.

"Yeah."

"That's great," Lisa smiled. "It's so wonderful to see young people that appreciate the library."

James looked around, still unsure about what punishment is about to come his way, but he muttered, "I guess so."

Lisa studied the anxious boy a moment before asking, "I was wondering if you might be willing to do a few odd jobs for me around here. It wouldn't take much of your time, but it would be a great help to me."

"Sure," he smiled, showing the large gap in his slightly oversized front teeth.

Over the next days and weeks, Lisa concocted several jobs for the boy. She was impressed by his diligence and after completion, he would always ask, "What's next, Miss Mathers?"

Lisa struggled at first, inventing work for him to do, but the young boy was an energetic worker and soon she had a list of odd jobs, which included sorting books and sometimes returning materials to the lower shelves. This routine went on through the summer, and James was a regular during the days the library was opened. When school began, James showed up most days after school. Lisa even had to drive the boy to school one day when he came to the library on a school day. To Lisa, the transformation had been remarkable, from the sneaky boy that tried to steal a book, to one who seemed to thrive on responsibility. James was more than a boy at the library now, he was her friend.

It was toward the beginning of the second nine weeks of school when Mrs. Jones showed up at the library to schedule a field trip. James tried to hide behind the periodical shelves in the back corner of the library, but Mrs. Jones spotted him.

"Miss Mathers," Mrs. Jones said. "I think we need to talk."

"What can I do for you?" Lisa smiled.

"I need a minute with you in your office, if possible," Mrs. Jones tersely replied.

For the next ten minutes, Mrs. Jones lamented about the sordid past of James Torrent. Mrs. Jones explained the boy had been in trouble since his first days at Horace Mann Elementary. He had been in fights, been caught stealing, and was a general disruption to the educational system. Mrs. Jones was "very concerned" to see the boy given so much free reign at the library. When Lisa argued it was hard for her to understand how a fourth-grader could be a "general disruption to the educational system," Mrs. Jones was emphatic and persistent that the boy was bad news. In short, Mrs. Jones warned that the library needed to be very careful with the boy.

Lisa had experience dealing with a wide variety of public concerns, but the ferocity of the teacher's accusations hit her personally. She had spent a lot of time with this boy, and he had reformed in her mind. She had taken a chance and seen a change.

"I'll take your concerns under consideration," Lisa tersely responded to the teacher. "But, I will have to judge James on how he conducts himself here at the library, not how I'm told he behaves in other places."

"Have I offended you?" Mrs. Jones replied.

"No," Lisa responded, although her answer is only a half-truth.

"I just wanted you to know," Mrs. Jones sighed. "I hope what you're saying about his work here is true. He comes from a tough family, and maybe this is a good place for him."

"I think it is," Lisa agreed.

After the teacher left, a sheepish James peeked into the office to ask, "What did Mrs. Jones want?"

"She's setting up a field trip," Lisa informed. "She said she had you in class last year."

"Yeah."

"She said—"

"She said I was one of the bad kids," James moped.

"No," Lisa quickly corrected. "She was—commenting on what good work you have done here. Is there a reason she might have said you were a 'bad kid?'"

James nodded pathetically, "I get in fights a lot at school and— I'm not that smart."

"I disagree," Lisa said. "Anyone that can navigate the Dewy Decimal System can—can conquer the world."

"You really think so?" James apprehensively asked.

"I know so," Lisa smiled. "How about you try a little harder at school and try to stay out of those fights?"

"Okay," James grinned with his gapped-tooth grin.

James continued to come to the library regularly the years Lisa worked at that downtown branch. As he entered middle school, he came by less often, but was still as excited as always to "help out" when he did come. Lisa left the downtown branch when James was twelve. He was a big boy then—almost a young man. He had to bend down to cry into her shoulder, and she promised she was not gone forever and would be back for visits.

Her new job managing a suburban branch of the library had its own challenges. She missed the old downtown library, but particularly she missed her "little helper." Life got hectic, but she did manage to return a few times. James was almost sixteen the next time she saw him. It was at the library. He had endeared himself to her replacement, as he had to her. He was a young man now and well on his way to being a handsome one. She asked about school, and he was still attending. She asked about the library, and he admitted he only managed to show up a couple of times a week, but always saw the library as a special place, just as she had when she was a girl. Lisa went back to her branch, and James continued with life, which now had a potential that was not so evident when he was a young boy stealing the books he could have borrowed.

Lisa's successful career continued. In a couple of years, she was asked to take a position at the main office to oversee system-wide programs and projects. It was a perfect fit for her. She missed the daily interaction with patrons she experienced at the branch level, but loved the implementation of new programs to help library users succeed. She even got used to hiring and sometimes having to fire employees. Lisa went back to school to earn a Master's of Business Administration and was on her way to implementing continuous improvement throughout the library system.

Her busy day was interrupted when Mrs. Jones knocked on the door of her office on a mid-week afternoon. Mrs. Jones was now serving as a vice-principal at one of the middle schools. Lisa had no idea why the woman had made her way to this office, but assumed she had a purpose.

"This is a surprise," Lisa greets. "What can I do for you?"

Mrs. Jones nods politely as she says, "By your greeting, I assume you don't know."

"Know what?" Lisa asks, in a somewhat more anxious tone.

"About James," Mrs. Jones answers.

"No," Lisa replies.

Mrs. Jones sighs, "James was shot last night in front of his house. He—he didn't make it. I thought you might have heard on the news last night."

Lisa feels the blood rush out of her cheeks, and the room seems to spin for an instant. How can this be? Lisa asks herself. She had heard about a shooting close to her old downtown library branch last night, but paid little attention. It seems as if there is bad news nearly every night, and she for the most part chose to ignore the details.

Lisa collapses into her desk chair as she asks, "How could this be? Are you sure?"

Mrs. Jones takes a seat and says, "I'm sure."

"I don't understand," Lisa sniffles. "I thought he was doing so well. I haven't kept up like I should, but this is—this is hard to process."

Mrs. Jones nods, "He was doing better in school. I think he would have graduated and considering his background that would have been amazing."

"What do you mean?"

Mrs. Jones takes a moment before saying, "James comes from a rough family. His mother is a well-known drug dealer in town, and who really knows who the father was. She's been in and out of jail. There always seemed to be characters around the house. It was a terrible place for a child, but there was enough family around to keep James out of foster care. The school knew some of it, but what can we do. We aren't the law."

Lisa is hesitant as she asks, "Was James involved?"

"I don't think so," Mrs. Jones quickly replies. "A car drove by and fired at the house. Someone inside returned fire. James was walking on the opposite sidewalk."

"What time?" Lisa asks.

"I don't know exactly," Mrs. Jones answers. "I think about 9:30 last night."

Lisa bows her head into her chest and mutters, "Right after the library would have closed."

"You're probably right," Mrs. Jones admits. "I think that was always the safe place for him. I thought you would want to know. I—I also thought you might want to know what a difference you made in his life."

"Thank you," Lisa manages to say.

Mrs. Jones excuses herself, leaving Lisa alone in her office. She struggles to believe the little boy that came so often to her library could now be gone. She had never thought or speculated much on his life outside of the library or why he had spent so much time there. Lisa sobs silently at her desk as she thinks of the lost potential. She had always considered the library her sanctuary, but she now understood in a very real way, it had been his sanctuary, as well.

THE END

CONFESSIONS OF A SALESMAN

Delores Selfridge was a woman who knew what she wanted and how to get it. She wasn't like other shoppers who wandered into the furniture store claiming, "I'm just looking." Delores always had a specific purpose to her shopping. She understood value and had a keen sense as to the best price on everything.

Anyone who has ever sold retail should get a degree in human psychology—or maybe at least some psychological treatment. When your job is to convince people to part with their money for something you have to sell, you understand their decision-making is cloaked in an incomprehensible shroud of emotion, ego, and triviality. One thing a salesman learns early on is that men and women are different. I've heard some of my more cynical sales professionals oversimplify the difference by concluding that men are rational and women are—crazy. This is not true. Men are just simpler in their buying decisions, while women tend to be more complex. I completely understand the above statement is not politically correct, but it is universally and historically accurate.

For example, a man discovers a hole in his shoe. He'll walk into a store, choose a black or brown color, buy the shoes, put on the shoes, and in less than twenty minutes, he no longer has a hole in his shoe—problem solved. For a woman, the process is exceedingly more intricate. First, she has to decide if only one pair of shoes could possibly replace her now outdated shoes. Then she'll have to decide the best time of year to buy. She'll do hours of research and shopping to carefully catalog every option. Next, she will need to bring in a host of advisors to critique and validate her opinions. After months of going through this process repeatedly and continually, she may buy a pair of shoes that will spend more time in the closet than on her feet. Shoe shopping is obviously a very complex process.

Although I would never want to be a shoe salesman (there is excessive drama and emotional commitment to footwear), selling furniture is no less taxing, and I would argue, has much more at stake. Men believe furniture is something to sit on, sleep on, or eat on. Of course, they could not be more wrong. For a woman, a furniture purchase is a statement of style, sensibility, and possibly their value as a human being. There is no less stress in the Super Bowl than for the poor woman who has to host her judgmental, out-of-state mother-in-law. Okay, that's slightly overstated, but for women, buying furniture is a bigger deal than for your typical man.

Through my years on the sales floor, I saw all kinds of customers. One of my personal favorites was the guy who showed up with his checkbook in his pocket needing a chair, a bed, and a television, because he had just been kicked out of the house by his woman. I feel badly for his relationship misfortune, but there was never an easier sale. Women are more social shoppers and rarely make a decision without bringing their cheerleaders—passive-aggressive "friends" who shroud jealousy with alleged helpful comments about style. When a woman brings her friend, you are no longer selling to the customer, but to the friend. Win that battle, and the commission check is all but yours.

I once had a customer choose the living room furniture of her dreams only to have her husband veto the deal while rudely criticizing her lack of sense and economy. He died of some strange food poisoning soon after. Two days after the funeral the woman returned to the store in a more pleasant disposition than seemed appropriate and promptly placed the order for her living room furniture. Some might have seen that as suspicious, but when selling furniture, you learn to not ask too many questions. None of my customers were ever as practical, ingenious, or successful as Delores Selfridge, however.

Delores, a meek-looking woman in her mid-fifties, came into the store nicely dressed with an air of prosperity that would make any salesman ask enthusiastically, "Can I help you?"

The answer to this question is always the same, "No. I'm just looking." Therefore, Delores looked. For almost an hour, she prowled the store, only occasionally asking a question, but her eyes were always moving like a predator in the wild. She gave a subtle nod that allowed me to approach as she stood over a handsome sofa located close to the main aisle.

"That's one of our best!" I chirp, in anticipation that she was close to making up her mind.

"It will do," Delores states with little emotion. "Tell me your best price."

I smile, "It's on sale for $599."

Delores sighs, not so much in agitation, but in resignation. "Young man," she begins. "I've shopped every store in a three-county area and know exactly the worth of this sofa. All I want is your best price."

I nod meekly at her kind scolding before sulking back to the sales manager's office to ask for a discount. Ed Boesky, the sales manager, was a barrel-chested man with years of experience making him volatile and temperamental to any young salesman daring to ask for a price concession. Knowing my request would come at the price of a stern lecture from my boss about the art of salesmanship, I reluctantly knocked on his door.

"Any chance we'll run that 685 England-Corsair sofa on sale soon?" I ask.

"What for?" Ed Boesky growls between bites of his morning donut. "It's one of our best sellers. You should know that. Go talk about the features and benefits—and whatever you do don't cower to the customer."

"I've got a lady interested," I groan. "She demanded I ask."

Ed frowns, "Cash or credit?"

"Cash—I guess."

Ed grimaces before asking, "Who's the customer?"

"Mrs. Selfridge," I answer.

Ed drops the donut and immediately straightens in his chair, "Delores Selfridge?"

"Yes," I confirm. "Is that a problem?"

"Not for you," Ed grunts, as he begins pounding on his worn calculator. "Sell it to her for $520."

"$520!" I exclaim. "There's nothing wrong with it. I've never known you to cave in so quickly. I haven't even met the husband yet."

"The husband doesn't really matter," Ed smirks. "Delores Selfridge is not your typical customer."

"Is she a problem?" I ask warily.

"Not Delores," Ed quickly clarifies. "In fact, she's been a very good customer for many years. She knows what she wants, is sharp on price—and she's fair—at least in her own way of thinking."

"What do I need to know?" I ask, somewhat intimidated by Ed's reaction to the lady on my sales floor.

"You don't need to know anything," Ed grins. "Delores will tell you exactly what to do."

I leave his office unsure and uncomfortable by my boss's vague reaction to giving a discount. Delores Selfridge seemed to be a harmless lady, but I could tell my sales manager had a healthy respect—almost fear of her. As I approached the middle-aged woman who seemed more affable than intimidating, I took a deep breath.

"I talked to my boss," I state factually. "He said you could have the sofa for $520." I don't wait for a response before adding, "That's the best price I've seen him give anyone on that piece. It's one of our best sellers—"

Delores interrupts me by simply putting up her hand as a signal for me to stop talking.

"That'll be fine," she announces.

"Great!" I smile. "When would you like it delivered."

"Not so fast," Dolores chides. "I'll have to bring Raymond in first."

"I thought we had a deal," I complain. "You asked for my best price."

"We do have a deal," she assures. "But, I'll have to bring Raymond into the store." She hesitates, "It's part of the process."

"Okay," I mutter.

"Be here Wednesday," Delores commands. "I'll bring Raymond in at ten o'clock. Take off all of the sales signs—make sure this piece is marked at the original, list price. You know, that price you'll never get."

"Okay," I nod.

"Raymond will not buy until you come down twice on the price," Delores coaches. "The first time he asks you for your best price, tell him $599. He'll fuss and fume before bullying you to come down on the price again. When he does, tell him $550, if he'll pay cash."

"I—I already told you $520," I remind.

Delores nods, "I know. You'll refund me the difference—me not Raymond. Those are my terms. Can you deliver?"

Somewhat confused, I moan, "I guess so."

Delores stares sternly at me, "You'd better know so."

"Yes, ma'am," I concede.

After Delores Selfridge leaves the store, I return to my sales manager's office for counseling and some advice about how to handle the strange request. Ed Boesky is not too sympathetic but congratulates me on the sale, which I'm not sure I've really made.

At ten o'clock Wednesday morning, Dolores Selfridge follows her husband, Raymond, into the store. Raymond is a more imposing figure than his wife, standing well over six feet, with a hardened physique indicating he was a man accustomed to hard work on the ranch he owned. Raymond does not seem happy to be in the store, but he is obviously in charge. As I start to approach,

I receive a subtle nod from Delores indicating it would be better if I let them look. It takes Delores only a few minutes to maneuver her husband to her chosen sofa before motioning me over to assist them.

"Is this the one you like?" Raymond bellows, in a harsh tone of voice that is somewhat frightening.

Delores nods, "It will do fine."

Before I can introduce myself, Raymond roars, "You work here?"

"Yes, sir," I reply.

"My wife's interested in this sofa," Raymond states. "I'm not so sure. We'll have to see how you can sharpen your pencil. What's your best price, and I mean your best price?"

I swallow hard as I look up at the imposing man. Everything in my being wants to say $520, as I had quoted his wife previously. As I look over at Delores, she gives me a reassuring nod as I manage to say, "It's only $599."

Raymond Selfridge looks like he might faint as he thunders, "Five—hundred—and—ninety-nine dollars! That's the best you can do? You better find some sharper lead in that pencil if you want to make a deal. My wife doesn't hate this sofa, but I'm not paying that."

I nod meekly as I say, "I'll go check and see what I can do."

Approaching the sales manager's office, I quickly discern that Ed Boesky is nowhere to be found. It doesn't really matter. He had already given me his advice on how to handle Delores. After a few minutes, I head back to my customer.

"I can do $550—cash," I say timidly.

Raymond Selfridge looks like a hard and demanding man, but he cannot contain his smirking grin as he says, "That's more like it!" Turning to his wife, he continues, "I told you he would come down again. See, I saved you nearly fifty dollars. That'll buy a nice meal out."

"Maybe Fitzgerald's," Delores suggests.

Raymond swallows hard as his grin becomes more grime as he mutters, "I guess so."

"That's wonderful," Delores gleams. "Why don't you pull the car around while I take care of the details?"

"Sure," Raymond grunts, as he nods at me.

"And, Raymond," Delores pleasantly reminds. "I'll need your checkbook."

Raymond hands a well-worn checkbook to his wife before turning to me to say, "Good doing business with you, and don't forget, we agreed on $550."

"Yes, sir," I concede.

As soon as her husband exits the store, Delores carefully and deliberately scripts a check for $550, plus the sales tax, while she gives me explicit directives on the delivery date, time, and her expectation of the deliverymen to avoid tracking any dirt onto her freshly shampooed carpets. She gives her instructions with a kind and patient demeanor, combined with a strange, intimidating power indicating I do not want to test her on violating even the slightest of her wishes.

Delores hands me the check and waits for only a second before asking, "Aren't you forgetting something?"

It takes me a moment to realize I owe her change. I've rarely, if ever, given cash back for a check, but do not argue that it was within our agreement. I quickly hand Delores thirty dollars, as she stares coldly at me.

"Is something the matter?" I nervously ask.

"You owe me two dollars and twenty-five cents for the difference in the sales tax," Delores states.

I'm caught by surprise, but immediately fumble to find the difference. When I hand the extra two dollars and twenty-five cents to her, Delores smiles with complete satisfaction at the transaction.

"Are we good?" I anxiously ask.

"Perfect," she replies.

As Delores Selfridge starts to leave, I'm compelled to say, "Can I ask you a question, Mrs. Selfridge?"

She stops and examines me thoroughly without answering for what seems like a minute before deciding to say, "You may."

"Do you negotiate many sales like this?" I ask.

Delores thinks before replying, "I suppose I do." I look at her and cannot work up the courage to ask the question I really want to ask. I don't have to as Delores continues, "I know you must think it's a strange arrangement, but I've been married long enough to learn a few things about my husband. When I was younger and more naive, I believed my husband should be in charge of certain things—that he should be the head of the house, and it was my job to support him. That didn't work very long. I learned Raymond, although a good provider and seemingly intelligent man, really didn't have much sense when it came to some things—I suspect he is like most men. The first few times I took him to stores for any sizable purchase, he would embarrass me by his constant haggling over the slightest discount.

"I soon realized that it was like a game to him. If the salesman would come down twice, he figured he had won. I also learned merchants would often come down on the price, and that was a good thing for me, it just didn't seem too efficient or pleasant. Through the years, I've learned the value of most things. I go in before Raymond and set up the parameters for success. It's important for Raymond to think he wins occasionally—to believe he's in charge."

"But he's really not," I deduce.

Delores laughs so softly it barely seems like a laugh as she says, "No man ever is—if he's with the right woman. Take today for instance. I could have brought Raymond without any preparation. Things would have gotten heated. Raymond would have become agitated if you gave him your best price the first time. It would not have been pleasant for you. Raymond makes a good living and knows the value of a dollar. It was the way he was raised. That's a good thing, but is it really worth it for a few dollars more? No, I've found it's better if I control the situation.

"You're happy, you've got your commission. I'm happy, I've got my sofa—plus thirty-two dollars and twenty-five cents and a very nice dinner out at Fitzgerald's with the money Raymond believes he has saved. It's important for Raymond to think he's in charge. It's good for his career, it's good for his business, and at the end of the day, it's important for me to know he's my puppet on a string."

I unintentionally smirk as I realize I've also been Delores Selfridge's puppet.

Delores looks at me carefully a moment before asking, "Are you a married man?"

"Yes, ma'am," I inform. "I've got a daughter and another on the way."

"Very good," Delores smiles. "We need good families, and you seem to be a nice enough young man. I'd like to give you some advice."

"Okay."

"Be patient with your wife," Delores continues. "Trust me, she's being patient with you. I've found life is better in a partnership. I don't know your wife and don't know what will work for her, but you're a team—or at least should be. Raymond is going to enjoy a nice supper with his wife, thinking it's with the money he bargained away from you. It's a nicer world when everyone wins—that's teamwork. Never believe you are easy to live with and never take your wife for granted."

"Yes, ma'am," I smile.

Delores Selfridge studies me carefully one more time before adding, "And make sure your deliveryman keeps every speck of dust off my clean carpets, or I'll have a conversation with your wife and explain to her how marriage should really work."

"Yes, ma'am," I reply.

Delores nods politely as she exits the store. Her husband rushes to open the door for her before speeding away. As soon as Delores is out of view, Ed Boesky reappears from the back of the store where I assume he's been hiding out.

"Is she gone?" Ed warily asks.

"Yeah," I sigh. "You were right. She was not your typical customer."

Ed smiles, "Some women know how to get what they want in this world—some more effectively than others. Heaven help the man that crosses that woman. I wish I could be as clueless as Raymond. He has no idea how much he's at the mercy of that woman. I wasn't so lucky. Delores looked up my first wife after a delivery guy tracked mud into her house. Delores might be a puppet master, but when she tried to teach my first wife how to handle a man, I wound up with the string around my neck with the ex-wife pulling with all her might. Learn from me. Never underestimate Delores Selfridge!"

THE END

JACK FULLER'S UNDERSTANDING

Jack Fuller managed the J. C. Penny store three doors down from where I worked. He was an older and distinguished-looking gentleman with silver hair. Taller than average, Jack dressed impeccably. He had a playful glint to his eyes and a constant smile. If he was not so lean and clean shaven, he would have been the perfect Santa Claus. Jack was probably in his sixties, but had the energy of a man much younger. He led the downtown merchants' association and came into the store a couple of times a month to talk about upcoming events, invite me to the next meeting of the association, or collect dues for a brochure the association published. Jack was an energetic conversationalist, and I enjoyed our visits on the days when business was slow.

I was twenty-seven-years-old when I first met Jack. Although we were from different generations, we had our common war stories of working retail and dealing with customers. As a college graduate with a business degree, I felt an obligation to share what I understood about modern sales and promotional techniques. Jack had years of experience, but it was clear he was not an educated man in the sciences and techniques of business marketing. I started as a salesman, but after a short time, worked my way into the position of merchandising and advertising manager for my father's store. Jack seemed to appreciate my philosophies about retail sales, and listened intently to my suggestions with his pleasant and easy smile.

After a time, Jack and I became more than acquaintances, and I considered him a friend. Of course, I was not Jack's only friend. He had been a fixture on Main Street for two decades before I began my career in sales. Everyone knew Jack, and he was universally liked, which I would learn was essential to being a successful merchant. I believed we had a connection. Jack encouraged me to join the Kiwanis club, and I learned he was even more passionate about Kiwanis than he was about the merchant's association.

During Jack's frequent visits to the store, he would ask about my baby daughter. We would talk about politics. His politics were conservative, as were mine, but Jack had a special patriotic fervor that went beyond any specific ideology. I managed to avoid any arguments about his decidedly old-fashioned ideals. We agreed on more things than not, and enjoyed a mutual respect, although I was a much younger man. Besides, we always found time to gripe about customers.

One day, I had a particular frustration with a Mrs. Johnston who had returned a table with some feeble excuse that made no sense. Jack smiled and explained he knew Mrs. Johnston well, and she was in the habit of returning nonreturnable items like worn pantyhose. His regional manager asked about the high number of hosiery Jack's location was returning. He had to have a conversation with Mrs. Johnston about her pantyhose. The thought of the distinguished Jack Fuller discussing a mature woman's pantyhose problems made me laugh-out-loud. I felt somewhat reassured knowing I was not alone in dealing with difficult customers. Jack let me know in his unassuming way that he had seen it all and even had to have a talk with a prominent attorney in town about occasionally fondling the mannequins in the lingerie department.

"You know the thing about customers?" Jack smiled.

"The customer's always right," I sighed.

Jack furiously shook his head, "No! No! No! I've been in sales thirty years, and I can tell you the customer is not always right. In fact, they are very often wrong, but the customer is always first. It's our job to make them feel like they are the most important people in the world when they're making a purchase."

I had never had one of my professors explain customer relations so eloquently, and I was beginning to understand I could learn a thing or two from Jack.

In the spring, the town buzzed when the local paper reported the J. C. Penny store had been robbed. Jack came by the store a few days later selling ad space in the association's summer brochure. I was eager to learn the details of the robbery, but found Jack unenthusiastic about the real-life drama.

"You need a pistol," I chided. "It takes minutes for the police to respond. You have a right to protect your property."

"Oh, no," Jack replied, while violently shaking his head. "I don't think that would be a good idea."

"But you were robbed," I reminded. "You don't want to be an easy target."

"Do you carry a gun?" Jack quizzed.

"Not with me," I frown, "but I'm considering it." Leaning in closer, I whispered, "We do keep a shot gun back by the counter."

Jack thought for a moment before asking, "For how long?"

"I don't exactly know," I confessed. "I've just seen it back there. It's granddad's gun. I'm not sure we even have the ammunition, but it could scare someone."

"Having a gun around is scary enough for me," Jack claimed.

"Come on," I argued. "You have to take a stand sometime. They have a night class on conceal and carry. Maybe you should consider taking one."

Jack shook his head, "No, not for me. I don't really like guns. Besides, have you ever thought how you would feel if you actually shot someone?"

I ponder his question before answering, "No."

"You would feel terrible," Jack surmised. "Better to let them take a few things than live with a lifetime of regret."

I disagreed and we politely argued for a few minutes, but Jack was not open to reason on the matter. As always, he left with a smile. Jack had long ago mastered the art of disagreeing agreeably.

My next encounter with Jack included the only scolding I ever got from him. My store decided to run a sale on Veteran's Day. It seemed sensible to me. Some people were off work, and it promised to be a good traffic day. Jack's admonishment was polite, but I could tell he was slightly disappointed in my plans for the promotion. He was an old-fashioned guy and patriotic. I considered myself a loyal American, as well, and rationalized it would be the American way to exercise some free enterprise for the holiday.

The place I saw Jack most frequently was at the weekly Kiwanis meeting. He had been the one that encouraged me to join. It was great for making contacts, and I even found it useful to have some fellow professionals with which to share my weekly stories. Jack sat with the "old guys" who took Kiwanis much more seriously than my group did. They were experts on Robert's Rules of Order, the history of the club, and the role the club held in the community. Jack's friends were serious enough to cause some of the younger members to smirk at their exuberant detail to the rules.

The club adopted the practice of having each member give a brief biography about themselves. I talked about my role in the business and related some of my accomplishments from college. Several weeks later, it was Jack's turn to share. I sat back to listen believing I would be entertained. In the next five minutes, I learned how little I really knew about the important things in life and marveled at this understated man who had been so generous to share his time with me.

Jack began with a few insults aimed at members of his table. He talked about going to high school somewhere in Kansas before stating humbly he worked the past thirty years for J. C. Penny—the last nineteen as store manager. Jack took great pride in his employment, and no one would ever question his loyalty to customers. He received the appropriate polite applause as he headed back to his seat.

Before Jack could sit down, one of the "old guys" at the table teased, "That's the most boring story I've ever heard! No one wants to hear about J. C. Penny. Tell 'em the real story."

"No one wants to hear about that," Jack smiled.

"Come on, Jack," one of the other men says. "Tell them about Guam."

Jack hesitates for only a moment before amiably returning to the podium.

"I don't know why you guys want to live in the past," Jack admonished. "I'm sure everyone's tired of my old stories."

"Not everyone's been around as long as dirt like us," the man joked. "Tell the story."

"I joined the army as soon as I turned eighteen," Jack began. "I'd been on the fringes of a few fights, but for the most part heard more about the war than actually seeing any of it. That all changed at Guam."

As Jack begins telling his story about his experiences in the war, I watch as his friends at his table listened intently. The teasing and joking vanished from the room. One could sense Jack had something to say, and everyone paid silent attention.

"We landed on day three," Jack continued. "I had heard the big guns from the ships before, but never sailing over my head. We had to wade and practically swim in from the reefs. When we finally made it to the beach, I saw bloody men everywhere. You get used to everything, I suppose, and pretty soon we were sent into action. We really couldn't see the Japs, but we could sure hear their bullets. I found a two-man foxhole about dark. Thinking about what was coming was worse than fighting. I dug like you've never seen a man dig before. I was sharing the hole with a sergeant from another platoon. Everything was messed up that first day. After dark, the sergeant went back for more ammo. He told me to stay awake. He said he'd shoot me himself if he came back and I was asleep.

"It was a dark, moonless night. All the sounds of the jungle were amplified. I was sure I could hear Japs all around. It seemed like hours in that hole by myself, not knowing if the sergeant was dead or alive. Out of nowhere, I heard steps coming from the opposite direction. I quit breathing and felt like time stood still. A second later, a Japanese soldier kind of fell into my foxhole. Fortunately, I had my rifle in my hand and squeezed three shots before I could think. I heard more steps running from the other side of the hole, and before I knew it, the sergeant jumped into the hole with me and the dead Jap.

"I've never been cursed like I was by that sergeant. He reminded me the Japs were all around and about to counterattack. He looked at the dead man crumpled in our foxhole as he continued to curse at me and told me I should have had sense enough to use my knife. The gunshot would make us a target.

"The sergeant was right about one thing. The Japs attacked with a vengeance. I fired my weapon for the next two days and nights until my finger was blistered. A machine gun nest had us pinned down. I spent two days looking at the dead man I had shot. When the tanks finally made it to the battlefield, and orders came for us to advance, I charged. I don't know if I would have been able to the first day, but after two days of looking at that body, I was ready to be somewhere else, even if that was the hereafter."

Jack hesitated a moment before looking at the old men at his table to say, "I can't believe you guys wanted to hear that story. When I went to the war, I was squeamish about anything dead. I fired my weapon a lot in Guam, but I never thought I'd have to stare at the man I killed for two days. I was lucky though. I survived Guam with only a single shot to the leg. My company went to

Okinawa in April, but I was back in a field hospital recovering. Good thing, too. The boys said Okinawa was a real fight."

The entire group of usually rowdy Kiwanians listened like they were at a funeral service. Jack did not seem affected by telling his harrowing story, but I sat in disbelief that he had endured such a hardship as a young man and had never bothered to share the story with me. I watch Jack leave the meeting, thinking how patient he had been with all of my silly stories.

I learned many things from Jack Fuller through the years. The most important thing was realizing you can never fully know or understand the totality of another person's life experiences and viewpoints, but you can respect everyone. Jack listened to my immature stories and philosophies with the full knowledge I was a young man trying to impress others at the start of my career. He was willing to listen and share his experiences knowing I had a chance of someday learning what he had during his long life. Jack Fuller had not always been able to convince me with his words, but he did by the way he led his life.

THE END

THE TOMBSTONE

All things in the universe work together in a manner sometimes hard to comprehend. Sometimes the confrontation with our minuscule place in the cosmos comes in surprising locations and the most mundane of times.

Roy and Martha were entering their golden years after 33 years of marriage. Their two children were grown, married, and on their way to successful lives of their own. One grandson from their thirty-year-old daughter, Leslie, and another from their twenty-seven-year-old son, John, had blessed the couple. Roy still worked, but had enough vacation time saved up to permit him a measure of leisure. The couple took an opportunity the few weeks before the hectic holidays for an overnight stay in Bartlesville. It had been a relaxing time for the couple, and they decided to explore the back roads home on a Saturday.

Their drive across the vast Oklahoma prairie led them through out-of-the-way towns like Pawhuska, Wynona, Hominy, Cleveland, Oilton, Drumright, Agra, and Chandler on their way home. It was a beautiful, crisp autumn day with a brilliant blue sky and comfortably cool temperatures.

After driving almost two hours, Roy spied a sign indicating they were approaching the town of Oilton. The small community was a shell of its former self. It had been one of those booming oil towns in the 1920s when some made fortunes and others lost lives. Years had passed since Roy thought about his grandfather on his mother's side, but something about the rusting welcome sign triggered his memory. Roy glanced over at Martha to see her quietly enjoying the repetitious countryside.

"My grandpa spent time in Oilton," Roy states dispassionately.

Martha straightens up in her passenger seat to survey the decaying town. "Your Grandpa Wills?"

Martha had only the vaguest memories of her husband's grandfather. He had been a sweet and feeble old man who attended their wedding, but passed away only a few months after their marriage. She had listened to family stories about him spending hours in a reclining chair reading his Bible, but knew little else about him.

"Yeah," Roy confirms. "He worked in the oilfields along the Cimarron River in the early twenties. He spent some time in Oilton, I think. In fact, his first wife is buried here."

"Your grandfather was married to someone before your Grandma Wills?" Martha quizzes.

Roy nods, "Yeah. My oldest aunt—Aunt Ruthie—was his first wife's child. She died in childbirth and is buried in Oilton. At least I think that's the story."

"I need to stretch," Martha claims. "Let's take a look." Martha surveys the small community before saying, "The cemetery can't be hard to find."

Close to the only gas station in town, the couple spied a worn and bent sign reading, "Cemetery."

Without comment, Roy turned up a narrow street that climbed a gentle hill about six blocks through a collection of homes that appeared to be constructed anywhere from the 1920s to the 1960s. Some were in good condition, but others looked abandoned. Two small towers fashioned as oil derricks, with the words "Highland Cemetery" welded in wrought iron spanning between them, guarded the city's graveyard. The size of the cemetery surprised them, appearing as if more people were dead than living in the small town.

"I guess this is it," Roy states the obvious.

Martha scans the larger than expected cemetery before saying, "Finding a single grave might be harder than we thought. Do you know where to look?"

"I have no idea," Roy confesses. "I've never been here. I know my grandfather worked around Oilton in the twenties so maybe there's some chronological order."

Roy parks their car toward the front of the cemetery near a majestic, old cedar tree. The late afternoon autumn sun cast an almost golden glow on the worn and weathered tombstones. The couple splits up and quickly surveys tombstones marking the lives of the people buried there.

After a few minutes of fruitless searching, Roy announces, "I'll call Mom."

Martha smirks at her husband finally coming up with such an obvious solution. She had been married to this man for more years than she had lived without him, but still marveled at his reluctance to ask for directions—even from his mother. Roy's mother answered and seemed somewhat excited that her son had taken the time to investigate some of the family's heritage. It was not a short conversation. Martha continued to grin playfully as her husband listened patiently to what she assumed was a conversation detailing the circumstances about his family's history.

Roy puts the phone away before saying, "She said it was south of the gate and close to an old cedar tree."

"That sounds like where we parked," Martha notes.

Roy nods and the two backtrack to the old cedar tree and quickly find the tombstone, which had been less than thirty steps from where they parked. They look down at the small marker in the middle of many other nearly forgotten monuments to lives past. The tombstone factually states:

PEARL I. WILLS

AUG. 21, 1904

DEC. 23, 1924

"Your grandfather's first wife had the same name as your grandmother?" Martha says, after a few moments.

"Yeah," Roy sighs. "I guess Pearl and Ruby and Opal were popular names back then."

"When was your grandfather born?" Martha asks.

Roy calculates before answering, "1898, I think."

"She was twenty," Martha says sadly. "He would have only been twenty-six. Do you know what happened?"

"Mom said Aunt Ruthie was born December 17th. Her mom had some kind of complication after the birth. I guess it happened a lot back then. These oil towns were pretty rough: a lot of desperate men looking to make a living for themselves and few doctors. She got some kind of infection, Mom thought."

Roy quits talking and shuffles around the gravesite, as if trying to get a perspective about something he is missing. Martha occasionally witnesses her husband in brief moments of sentimentality and senses this is one of those times. They originally stopped at this obscure little cemetery intending to stretch their legs, but she knows something's on her husband's mind.

"What are you thinking?" Martha finally asks.

"About what?" Roy sniffles defiantly.

Martha did not respond immediately, but then says, "About this place, I guess."

Roy looks at his wife and nods slightly.

"Grandpa never liked Christmas, much," Roy begins. "I see why, now. He would have stood here—maybe at this very spot on Christmas Eve, having lost the wife of his youth and holding a baby not even two weeks old." Roy looks around the cemetery before continuing, "It would have been brown and bleak in December. This old cedar might have been the only color in the whole countryside that day. This old tree looks like it's been here since the beginning of time. I bet it didn't look much different then and—my grandfather stood here having lost everything in his wife and holding everything in his daughter. He was twenty-six years old. That's a year younger than our son John. Can you imagine John standing here under those circumstances?"

"I can't, and I don't want to," Martha groans.

Roy is silent for a few seconds before adding, "My grandpa was always an old man to me. It's hard to imagine he was once young. He'd been to the Great War before coming to the oilfields. I knew that, but it's never seemed real before—at least not this real. He went back to Missouri—near Monett—where family could help with Ruthie. His first wife's family was more well-to-do than his clan and blamed him for taking their daughter away to live in a place like Oilton. Mom says it was a bad time. They didn't want much to do with him or Ruthie. They said it reminded them too much of the daughter they had lost.

"Grandpa's cousin took the little girl in to help him out. Grandpa did odd jobs, but times were hard. After a year, the cousin prodded him to return to the oilfields. He could make money back in Oklahoma, but there was no way for him to take care of his daughter. The relatives wanted him to leave Ruthie behind. They offered to adopt the girl, but she was all he had left.

"A neighbor girl helped the family with Ruthie and was good with the baby. She was only seventeen, but old enough to marry and without better prospects. My grandparents married and moved back to Oklahoma—with Ruthie."

"Your Grandma Wills was the girl?" Martha asks.

Roy nods with a grin, "I guess you could say it was a marriage of convenience, but they had six more kids on their own and were married nearly sixty years, so—I guess there was something more than babysitting going on."

Martha chuckles at her husband's assessment while moving to hold his hand. "This is an important place and time to you."

"It was to my grandpa, I guess," Roy concedes. "I still can't imagine what a terrible day that must have been."

"You don't get it," Martha clarifies. Martha organizes her thoughts before saying, "We're all caught in a circle of life. We're born, we live, we die. It's inevitable." Surveying the cemetery,

Martha explains, "All of these tombstones represent that circle of life. Each of these markers is a testament to the birth, life, and death of each person here. Many lived lives too short and some lived to ripe old ages. What matters is how they lived while they were here. I never knew the woman buried under this tombstone, but I believe she was loved. She gave birth to a girl that was sweet and good. Your aunt had three children of her own that would not be here if not for this woman. She died, and that is tragic, but look at what was gained."

"I guess," Roy sighs.

"You're still not seeing the point," Martha chides. "If this woman had lived—if your grandfather had not endured this tragedy—my world would be upside down. My life would be nothing like what I've enjoyed so much the past thirty-three years."

"You've lost me," Roy huffs. "This was a very bad day for Grandpa. I can almost see a twenty-six-year-old man looking much like my son grieving this loss, but how does that turn your life upside down?"

Martha puts her hands on her husband's cheeks as she explains, "Without this tragedy, your grandfather would have never gone back home to Missouri. He would not have met your grandmother. Your mother would not have been born—at least not exactly like she became. You would not have been born! We would have never met, and if I did have two children they certainly wouldn't be the same children we've raised, and loved, and cherished. Everything is connected. If your grandfather had not had a terrible Christmas Eve all those years ago, nothing would be the same. I love this woman that I never had the chance to meet.

I'm sorry she died so young, but I don't regret it. Look at what became of your grandfather's tragedy."

"I never thought about it that way," Roy stammers. "I guess everything that happens to us, takes us to where we are."

"And everything that happened to our ancestors has made us what we are," Martha adds. "Let's go home."

"Why the hurry?" Roy asks.

Martha smiles, "I want to look at pictures of my kids when they were young. I want to call them on the phone and see how the grandkids are. I want to cherish all that I have, because of what happened here in 1924. I want to make sure I live my life as best I can."

Roy nods and moves to the car. He takes one final look at the ancient cedar tree guarding the tombstone his grandfather had placed those many years ago. As he starts the car and begins to pull out of the cemetery drive, he says, "I never expected to find such an important place here."

THE END

TALE OF TWO CATS

Gladys Lazenby discovered she was a cat person fairly late in life. It was after her youngest son married. His bride gave her a calico kitten from the rescue shelter. Gladys smiled and graciously accepted the gift with false enthusiasm and pleasantness. She had kept pets when her children were young: a couple of dogs, a black cat they inherited when they moved into their house, and later a cat they kept outside to battle a single mouse she had seen in the yard one afternoon. Those pets were all loved, but gone. Gladys and her husband Bill prepared for their son's wedding and looked forward to having the house to themselves when she received her newest feline gift.

The kitten was small and weak, demanding more attention than Gladys imagined. Gladys was softhearted, however, and after a few days, she became attached to the cat, which she named Callie. To Gladys's surprise, her sometimes-grumpy husband liked the cat as well. Callie came from an animal shelter, where someone, at some time, had de-clawed her. All her previous pets had been strictly banished to the outdoors. On extremely cold or stormy nights, Bill might allow a pet in the screened porch or garage, but never inside the house. That was Bill's rule. He was stubborn and dogmatic about it until Callie came to the home. In the early days of Callie's addition to the household, the kitten would climb into Bill's lap before snuggling against his neck as they both napped. There was no discussion, no decision-making process, but by mutual affirmation, Callie became an inside cat.

Gladys and Bill did not know they were cat people, but the arrangement worked well in the large home now void of children. Bill adapted quicker than Gladys believed possible to the idea that you don't own cats, they own you. Bill would play with the cat a few minutes in the evenings, and Callie was content to nap in the comforts of the home the rest of the day. Gladys wondered if her husband secretly wanted to be a cat. He liked to snack all day, was prone to bursts of creativity and activity before taking habitual afternoon naps. The orphaned cat hit the jackpot when given to Gladys. The arrangement worked well. Callie had no claws to damage her furniture, and with several rowdy dogs in the neighborhood, Gladys only let her outside under close supervision. The rest of the time, Callie owned the inside of the house...in many ways more than Gladys and Bill.

Life for Callie was ideal. Of course, she would have liked to have the freedom to explore the backyard. When she was not napping, she would often gaze longingly outside, watching the birds and the blue sky. Her pillow by the window was soft, however, and many days the skies were gray. Callie was content to be an indoor cat. She would play a few minutes with Bill in the evenings, pick at her food periodically during the day, and nap most of the rest of the time.

Callie's utopia shattered in a most unexpected way and circumstance. Gladys's ear-piercing scream alerted the cat to the fact all was not well in the Lazenby house. Callie thought little of it at the time, but it would affect her life forever. Gladys had found a mouse in her kitchen. The woman scolded Callie in a way the cat did not understand, before weeping to her husband. Parts of the house were shut off to Callie and little wood traps were placed in out-of-the-way locations. More disconcerting to Callie was a stray cat prowling around the back fence of the yard in which she was not allowed. It was all very stressful to the cat, so she took a nap.

Callie awoke to a frightful sight. The stray cat from the backyard was now in the house. It was a pathetic display. Gladys held the stray on her lap and embarrassingly caressed its neck. Seems this outdoor cat had killed a mouse and dropped the carcass by the back door. Very uncouth, Callie thought. This outdoor cat had no business inside. It was a shaggy thing with no manners and darting, suspicious eyes. Why is Gladys holding this loathsome animal from the outdoors? Her hands will certainly be too dirty to rub my back. Fortunately, Gladys had the sense to send the outdoor cat away, but not before putting a bowl of food and water by the door. Not surprisingly, this outdoor cat hung around the backyard like bad company.

The outdoor cat brought a dead bird to the door the next day. Callie smirked, in that stoic way cats have, knowing this would be the end of the fiend that had invaded her home. Gladys would take her broom to the stranger, and life would finally return to normal. Unbelievably however, Gladys gave the outdoor cat only a mild scolding, sent the man to bury the dead bird, and gave the despicable outdoor cat a treat before picking her up to gently massage her neck. To add insult, when Gladys came back, she tried to pet Callie with the same hand she used to touch the outdoor cat.

Callie was insulted, and showed as much, as she sashayed away for an afternoon nap.

The nightmare escalated over the next several days. The outdoor cat killed a second mouse, which sent Gladys into a relieved ecstasy as she sent the man out to bury the tiny mouse. The outdoor cat received another treat before the unthinkable happened. Gladys picked up the outdoor cat and carried the mangy beast inside.

"You're a mouser!" Gladys exclaimed, in a surreal voice that one would use with a small child. "Yes, you are!" Gladys continued. "You're a little vagabond, you are. I'm going to call you Bonnie, you little vagabond!"

Callie could not let this stand. She hissed at the new cat. She fluffed her tail up angrily to show her disgust. The vagabond…this Bonnie, just watched innocently, as Callie hissed and fluffed. As soon as Gladys left the room, Bonnie growled evilly, while showing her devilish claws that allowed her to mercilessly hunt the mice Gladys so despised. Callie snarled back, trying to intimidate the stranger, but the scary outdoor cat was bigger and fearless. Callie rejoiced when Gladys returned, but instead of tossing the trespasser out the door, the woman shut Callie in a room and let Bonnie play inside.

The game was over. Gladys and Bill had somehow been duped, in Callie's opinion, into having two cats. Bonnie was taken to the vet. Callie was sure that indignity would cause the free-spirited Bonnie to flee, but she did not. Over the next several weeks, a pattern emerged where Callie spent her days inside while Bonnie was exiled to the outdoors. When Bill came home in the evening, however, Bonnie was let inside the house. Callie would be allowed a few minutes outside before being sequestered to the other side of the house. Her fuming at Bonnie, who frolicked playfully in the great outdoors, ruined Callie's former pleasant life.

The weeks turned into months of this new routine. Callie's life was miserable. Before, she had spent leisurely hours napping on her silk pillow by the window. Now that time was interrupted by watching Bonnie have something she did not have—the freedom to be outside. Worse, when Bonnie was let inside to invade her domain, Gladys would shut off the house to let Callie have one side and Bonnie the other. Callie hated closed doors and spent much of her time trying to look underneath the door to hiss at Bonnie if she were near to the door.

What Callie did not understand was how much Bonnie resented being the outdoor cat. Bonnie knew she was exiled to the outdoors for much of the day, while that inside cat lounged lazily on her pillow by the window—mocking the poor outdoor cat. Sure, the outdoors had its adventures, but many days it was too hot and other days it was too cold. There were barking dogs next door she had to contend with, and there were always birds or squirrels or mice that she had to hunt. From Bonnie's perspective, Callie had no idea how hard the outside world could be.

So, life became routine for the two cats. Callie was resentful she had to share any of the attention she previously enjoyed with this outdoor cat. Meanwhile, the leisurely and lazy life of Callie's indoor sanctuary made Bonnie increasingly jealous. Gladys hoped her two cats might someday be friends, but there was little evidence of that happening. Callie continued hissing and fluffing her tail at the intruder, while the bigger Bonnie often chased the indoor cat, causing frequent ruckuses. Gladys resolved herself to love each cat in her special, yet different way. Callie was shut up in the house during the day, and Bonnie was let into the house only a few hours each day, but always slept on the porch.

It's hard to determine if it was coincidence or fate, but on the same day, the indoor cat and the outdoor cat decided to make a change in their living arrangement. When Bonnie was let in for her evening time in the house, she found a secret hiding place. When Callie was allowed her time outside, she decided to explore far away from the porch, with the intention of shunning her inside prison. When darkness fell, Gladys frantically searched for the inside cat hiding outside and then the outdoor cat hiding inside.

Bill was sent into the night to hunt for Callie, but she had concealed herself in the neighbor's backyard and easily evaded him. Bill did not look long, and soon shrugged, before returning to the house. Gladys came next, pleading for Callie to come to the door, but the indoor cat was determined to have her freedom this evening—just like her nemesis Bonnie enjoyed every night.

Gladys eventually located Bonnie's hiding place under the sofa. Gladys marveled that a cat as fat as Bonnie could fit in the small place. She scolded the cat mildly before rubbing Bonnie's tummy, which was the cat's favorite treat. Bonnie assumed she would be exiled to the outdoors like she had every other night since taking up residence in this yard. Tonight, however, was different. Gladys was frenzied with worry. She muttered something about avoiding a backyard brawl in the night. To Bonnie's delight, Gladys allowed her to spend the night inside because Callie escaped outside.

Bonnie's euphoria was short lived. After her tummy rub, she decided to lounge on Callie's soft pillow positioned by the window looking outside. The pillow was soft and the view grand, but after a time, Bonnie became bored. As she viewed her backyard, she became increasingly agitated. She could not stalk the squirrels or trap the birds. All she could do was watch. The pillow was permeated with the essence of Callie, and she could not stand that for long. She decided to stretch and explore. The sofa had been a great place to hide. It was usually the room Callie was sent to when Bonnie made her nightly visits, but tonight the entire house belonged to her. The sofa was soft and tall. She first rubbed up against it before gently caressing the fabric with her paws. The material felt smooth and made a wonderful sound as her claws scratched on it. The noise was enough to attract the attention of Gladys.

The reaction of the woman was quite unexpected by Bonnie. Gladys sighed and screamed at the same time. She moved quicker than Bonnie thought possible and roughly scooped the cat away from the sofa. Gladys muttered angry words, which Bonnie did not understand, but believed they were targeted at her for some reason.

Bonnie could not help but notice she was under constant surveillance now. Even the subtlest move toward a piece of furniture elicited a quick response by Gladys or Bill. This ballet continued for a time, before Gladys announced it was time for bed. The woman lamented that she could not find Callie and did not want both cats outside where they might fight. Bonnie understood Gladys was distraught at Callie's absence, but that did not prepare her for what came next.

Gladys took Bonnie to a small back room and put her into a smaller cage. There was plenty of room to lie down, and the cage was comfortable but still confining. Bonnie had her special place on the ground at the corner of the house where she had spent most nights the past few months. A screened vent blew warm air when it was cold. In the summer, a cool stone sat in the shade all day providing the perfect spot to lie if it were warm outside. It was her place and she felt protected, but still free to roam the vast backyard. This cage was like—a prison. Worse than that, the cage, like the pillow, smelled like Callie! Bonnie quickly determined this would be a long night. She planned her escape and decided to take the first opportunity that presented itself to bolt outside.

Callie felt quite satisfied having eluded Bill, and later, Gladys. They had denied her this freedom far too long, and she was easily able to resist their pleas to come inside. The house appeared much different from this vantage point. The light glowed through the window in the dark night. As Callie surveyed her surroundings, she was suddenly concerned about the vastness of the outdoors. It was dark, which was no issue with her nocturnal feline vision, but there was a creepiness to the still night. She felt vulnerable and exposed as she cowered underneath the bush where she had been hiding. Looking into the house, she became agitated and then angry as she watched Bonnie sitting in her window seat—on her silk pillow—peering out at this dangerous outdoors.

Callie's great outdoor adventure soon became her nightmare, as the sounds of the night surrounded her. An old tomcat, three houses down, snooped around before hissing at her. The squirrels and the birds Bonnie enjoyed hunting annoyed her, but when a cagey raccoon forced its way under the fence, Callie sprinted for the house. Bonnie watched her from the comfortable seat in the window, but showed no concern. Callie purred and meowed as loudly as she dared, but the house was now dark, and she was all alone in this wilderness. Even Bonnie was gone, and Callie felt anxious vulnerability and abandonment. She wanted to sleep so badly—it was really all she was good at—but the night sounds and the unknown made it impossible for her to relax for a second.

It was a long night and just before dawn when she heard the click of the back door unlatch. Callie had heard this disconcerting sound many times when Gladys would usher Bonnie inside the house. Callie barely heard the woman exclaim, "There you are!" as she scampered into the warm and safe home. Callie tried hard to not seem too excited, but she anxiously kept an eye out for her archenemy Bonnie. Gladys caught her by total surprise when the exuberant woman slid her hand under the cat's belly and gently cuddled her while rubbing her chin. Callie purred with pure delight. She was back where she belonged.

"I missed you!" Gladys gasped, in her exaggeratedly loving voice she liked to use. "I was worried sick! Silly cat. How did you run off without me noticing? I had to keep poor Bonnie inside all night."

In her joy, Gladys forgot her other cat was shut up inside the back bedroom. She gently placed Callie on her silk pillow before retreating to the back of the house. Callie stretched and surveyed her familiar surroundings before kneading her pillow the way she liked and curling into a ball. Her special spot still had the faint stench of Bonnie, but she was too tired to care. In a few moments Gladys returned, toting Bonnie lovingly in her arms. Callie would generally hiss at the outdoor cat, but this morning she did not have the energy. Besides, she no longer wanted to trade places with Bonnie. For her part, Bonnie seemed content to take her place outside. Bonnie enjoyed the comforts of the indoors and Callie's pillow perched by the window, but she had her own pillow on the porch. She was an outdoor cat and was anxious to get back to chasing squirrels, birds, and mice.

Bonnie was ready for her freedom. She had been envious of Callie, but no more. Living indoors was too confining. From that day forward, Callie was more careful to stay close to the house and not get lost outside. She cherished the comforts of her indoor life. Gladys continued to love both cats as much as she could. She realized her cats were different, and it was her job to make sure both enjoyed their lives. After that night, the indoor cat and the outdoor cat determined Gladys really did know what was best for them. Bill had known that for a long time. After watching his wife take diligent care of the cats, Bill believed he might enjoy a cat's life. He wasn't sure he could catch a mouse, but was already an expert at taking naps.

THE END

THE WOMAN THEY CALLED MOM

Solomon said, "Kind people benefit themselves." I did not learn this with my expensive university education. Like most important lessons in life, I had to learn this by observation.

After completing college, I took a job with an accounting firm to pay my dues and start my journey to success. A portion of paying my dues involved renting a shabby house in a neighborhood beneath my past and future station in life. It was necessary, and as an up-and-coming young professional, I understood this neighborhood would be a temporary humility that would someday become a footnote to my inevitable memoirs detailing my success. I found myself feeling sorry for my neighbors who were at the pinnacle of their potential, living in this unimportant and borderline depressed part of town.

One woman particularly, symbolized this quagmire of lower middle class. She was an older woman living across the street from me. I never bothered to know her name or introduce myself. She would wave—and smile—when I would occasionally see her from the front porch. I was obligated to return the greeting, but our relationship never evolved beyond this forced interaction.

I found myself sometimes resenting this nice woman for no other reason than she made me uncomfortable and reminded me of the mediocrity in life I feared. Fortunately, I was busy enough with work and life that I never had to cross the street and discover the many failures of her life that destined her to such a mundane existence in this most common of neighborhoods.

My career was everything my poor neighborhood lacked. I managed to find an internship, and later, a job in one of the best accounting firms in the state. You could feel the drive for success the moment you stepped through the doors. Professional dress, high energy, and pure ambition drove the firm. All of the worker bees, like me, focused on proving ourselves.

I was thrilled when assigned to my boss's team. She started at the firm as a clerk, but worked her way up to full partner. Although not as polished as some of the other partners, she had a reputation as a no-nonsense supervisor who achieved results regardless of the circumstances. I was thrilled to be under her. The junior members of the firm understood she had an outstanding track record of moving her protégés through the firm quickly toward an eventual partnership position. She may not have had the same charisma that some of the other partners possessed, but she seemed to be comfortable in her skin.

Months went by and seasons changed, but my total focus was on work. Occasionally I would see the woman across the street on the weekends, but never bothered more than a congenial and generous wave. I would see people come in and out of the old, rundown house, but they never stayed long. I assumed they were the woman's grown children, but I wasn't interested. She appeared to live alone so I assumed she was widowed or divorced. It didn't really matter to me. I saved some of my salary and planned to move to a better address soon.

I purposely ignored the comings and goings of the across-the-street neighbor. I managed to avoid crossing that street until I saw my boss's new luxury car parked in front of the neglected house. I quickly straighten my clothes and assume she is here to see me— possibly to give me the good news of a promotion or an important assignment to advance my career. I wave when she sees me, and she returns the gesture before walking slowly toward my neighbor's house.

My residential street is narrow and never busy, so I take the opportunity to investigate. I assume my boss knows my neighbor someway, and I cannot resist the chance to socialize with the boss.

"Hello, Sam," my boss greets, as she stands at my neighbor's door. "I didn't know you lived here."

"A few months," I smile. "I'm surprised to see you."

"Just came by to see, Mom," she replies.

"Your mother lives here?" I say, trying hard not to gasp.

How could this be? I think to myself. This doesn't look like the part of town where the mother of a successful partner of my firm would live. How could I have not known this? Why hadn't I taken the effort to know my neighbor? This could have been good for my career!

A more sobering thought then crosses my mind. Not only have I never met my neighbor, the mother of my boss, I've been borderline rude and certainly condescending in my attitude. My boss is going to know. I will no longer be on the fast track to success. I'll be lucky to have a job.

"Well, she's the woman I call Mom," My boss explains. "I've tried to convince her to move, but she won't leave the old house."

Before I have a chance to retreat, the door creaks open and my neighbor comes out to greet my boss with a hug.

"I had no idea you were coming!" my neighbor says. "This is a great surprise!"

"Thought I needed to check up on you," my boss says. "I didn't know you were neighbors with my employee."

I brace for the worst, but instead, my neighbor says, "Sam's a dear. He's been such a good neighbor to me. But—you really are working him too hard. A young man needs some time off to socialize! You should look into that."

"I will Mom," my boss smiles.

"I better let you two enjoy your visit," I say, as I dismiss myself from this awkward reunion.

"Nonsense," my neighbor insists. "At least come in for a cup of coffee—and I've made cookies."

"You won't want to miss out on Mom's cookies," my boss adds.

I'm caught with no choice, but to enter the old house for coffee and cookies. Vivian, which I learned was my neighbor's name, quickly puts me at ease. The inside of her house is no more impressive than the outside, with a collection of old furniture and keepsakes, which are on the edge of being antiques, but without any hope of being valuable. I end up spending two hours in "Mom's" home.

I learn Vivian is only ten years older than my boss is. She took on the responsibility for two younger children that belonged to a former boyfriend when she was only twenty. My boss came from a troubled home when she was fourteen, and Vivian became her default foster mom when she was only twenty-four. Over the years, Vivian had been foster mom to scores of kids and adopted six of them.

Vivian sacrificed continuing her education, starting a career, or getting married to take care of her kids. As she would say, "All kids need a chance. I couldn't do everything, but I could do that." She had seen a couple of her kids through college. One had become a successful building contractor, and most of the others had found their place in life. Her crowning achievement was ten grandchildren all with the chance to live in a good home. My neighbor Vivian had managed to make quite a mark on her world and the lives of the many kids she had "taken a chance" on.

I excuse myself and return to my house, feeling better for knowing Vivian, but guilty for the way I had judged her, knowing I had ignored her for months. It was later in the afternoon, when Vivian walks across the street toward my house.

"Hello, Vivian," I greet.

"I wanted to apologize for dragging you into our old family stories this afternoon," she smiles. "I imagine you had some better plans for your day off."

"Not really," I frown. "Why did you do it?"

"Do what?" Vivian asks.

My shoulders slouch as I answer, "You acted like we were close neighbors in front of my boss, today. You know as well as I do that I've never bothered to cross that street until today. I've—I've not been a good neighbor, and—I think you probably know that. Still, you treated me like I was someone special in front of your daughter."

"I think everyone's special in their own way," Vivian smiles. "Your boss is smart—I knew that from the first time I met her when she was a too-big-for-her-britches teenager. I imagine she can be a handful at work. It never costs anything to be nice, and I thought you might like to know a little about her and what makes her the way she is."

Vivian studies me a second before saying, "I've never ventured over here, either, so I guess we could both improve on our hospitality. I stay pretty wrapped up in my kids. Sometimes I forget there's a bigger world out there beyond my yard. I'll tell you what. I'll come over and visit more, and bring you some cookies."

I try not to react, but Vivian watches me carefully as she grins, "I'll just come for a visit. I know my cookies aren't that good. They're just flour and sugar, but my kids all loved them growing up, and I still make them the same way."

As Vivian starts to walk across the street, I say, "Why don't you bring me some of those cookies next time, Vivian. Like you said, everyone—and everything—needs a chance. I bet I learn to love them as much as everyone else."

I had seen Vivian before that day, but never really noticed her before. She was just another old woman that lived in my neighborhood—unremarkable in every way. I never invested the time to notice this amazing woman living so close to me. I took her for granted and learned it was always a mistake to judge someone before taking the time to know them. She touched many lives for the good with her simple, unassuming ways, and I wondered if I could ever hope to accomplish so much.

Solomon also said, "A kindhearted woman gains honor, but ruthless men gain only wealth." It makes me wonder if old

Solomon knew someone like my neighbor Vivian—a woman that so many kids "that just needed a chance," called Mom.

THE END

A TITANIC DESTINY

Extraordinary—almost supernatural stories happen to other people all the time, but not to an ordinary guy like me. I live with a phobia I will someday be faced with a crisis that will reveal me as a hero or a coward. I like to think I would be brave, but one can never know until the unexpected occurs. I fear I might shirk from any semblance of courage.

I live a simple, uneventful, and sometimes tediously average life. I work as a landman searching the archives of out-of-the-way courthouses to determine property ownership so my company can make offers on land leases to drill for oil and gas. I don't actually produce any oil or gas; I simply search the property records to get a glimpse of other people's good fortune. I live in a rundown house in the historic district of the Paseo in Oklahoma City. A historic district is a fancy way of saying old and worn-out. The house creaks in the wind and smells of the old people that used to live there. It's a rental, but suits my purposes.

I do have one extraordinary thing in my life—Mary Louise McAnally. Mary is half Irish, half Cherokee, and one-hundred percent perfect. She exudes energy, spirit, and a zest for life that everyone immediately recognizes the minute they meet her. She is way out of my league, but introduced herself into my life, and I adore everything about her.

Mary is a third-year medical student. Most students buckle under the pressure of clinical rotations, but Mary thrives. I spend my days sniffing through dusty abstracts while she saves lives. She wants to be a pediatrician—and unbelievably she wants me. I have no idea why, but it is the astonishing thing in my life.

We plan to marry in the summer. Mary insists on a small and simple wedding, which is fine with me. There's only one catch to my perfect relationship—the future in-laws. Not that I have met them yet, because I haven't. I've come up with enough excuses to frustrate a less patient fiancé, but my Mary is as understanding as she is beautiful.

I have nothing against her family, but I have painful memories of my own. I never knew my father. He ran out on us and turned my mother bitter against men—and the world. I was a painful reminder of the man that stole her youth. She was never particularly kind or patient, but I still cried when she passed away shortly before my twelfth birthday. Several aunts and uncles tried to raise me, which causes me to relate drunken arguments as a staple to any family gathering. I bounced around foster care for most of my teen years, but finally hit the jackpot when an uncle of my mother took me in. Uncle Earl was old and wobbly. I took care of him about as much as he took care of me, but he was the best thing to happen in my life—until Mary. Uncle Earl gave me discipline and direction when I needed it the most. Uncle Earl did something even more important for me. He believed in me and challenged me to do better. He was not a man of means, but when he died my senior year of high school, he left a small life insurance policy to help pay for most of my college expenses. I graduated without distinction and have been on my own since then.

My biggest angst in meeting Mary's family is the genuine fear they will realize I am not worthy of her. They would be right, of course. Mary is too good for me, but then she's too good for anyone. I want more than anything to love and support her. I imagine if I don't make a powerful first impression, they will try to convince her to wait until after med school for a serious relationship. I have confidence in Mary's stubbornness, but I don't want her to have to live with the nagging reality that her family does not approve. I feel a tickle in the back of my throat. With any luck, I'll have a fever and avoid the meeting with the future in-laws. Mary has Monday off, and spending the weekend in my drafty house with her nursing me back to health sounds like the perfect medicine.

I watch a Sunday documentary about Titanic on the *National Geographic* channel in a semi-conscience daze. Titanic, and any disaster, has always fascinated me. The program does not have my full attention, however, and I find myself dozing on the couch. When I hear Mary's little Pontiac in the driveway, I rush like a puppy dog to watch her walk up the three steps leading to the front door. I open it before she gets there and hug her on the front porch.

"I don't know if I'd hug these scrubs so tight," Mary says, as she leans her head into my neck.

"Hard day?" I ask, as I continue to wrap my arms around her.

"A kid threw up on me," Mary replies.

I immediately release her and take half a step back.

Mary smirks, "I changed clothes before I left the clinic."

I nod and resume my hug.

"I did help deliver a baby in these, though," she whispers in my ear. "There may be something worse than vomit on them now."

"I don't care," I say, as I continue to pull her gently against me.

"I'm glad, Jeff," Mary sighs, as she seems content to lean against me and let me hold her. "How about I use your shower before we hit the road?"

I step back before sighing, "Have you seen the weather?"

"Yes," she smiles. "Maybe some thunderstorms, but it is April in Oklahoma. It's less than three hours to Tahlequah. If you'll load your things in the car and leave me alone, we'll be at Mom and Dad's by nine."

"We could call and delay," I suggest. "You have an extra day off, and I've got a tickle in my throat."

Mary tilts my head back to look in my mouth.

"You'll live," she states. "And we're going tonight. It has to be this weekend."

The weekend is almost over, and I would like to argue, but I have no case. Mary knows it as she grins sweetly.

"Are we taking your car or mine?" she asks.

"Mine," I concede.

"Good," she smirks. "I've got my travel cloths in my duffle. I'll shower and change then we can go. The rest of my bags are in the back seat. I'll race you to see if you can load the car quicker than I can change."

As we walk into the front room, Mary notices my documentary.

"Learning about Titanic?" Mary smirks.

"It was on," I alibi. Mary knows I'll watch or read anything about the tragedy. "It's a little different take. Someone's claiming the ship was switched, and it was actually her sister ship Olympic that went down. They theorize J. P. Morgan pulled the switch to collect insurance money."

"But the ship still sinks, right?" Mary teases.

"Yeah," I smile.

I load the car while Mary changes from her scrubs. She, of course, gets her way. I knew she would, and I don't really mind. The three-hour drive will go by too quickly, and then I'll face the inevitable disapproving father.

Traffic coming out of the city is hectic, but soon we clear the urban congestion and roll into the rhythm of a country drive. Mary tells me more about her day. She asks about mine. She turns the radio up when one of our favorite songs plays, and the trip is going way too fast for me. I could drive in the car with Mary forever. We can talk about anything, and my world seems right when I'm with her.

When we exit the interstate for the last hour of our drive it's dark, and I ask the question that has been on my mind since Mary planned this trip. "Will your parents like me?"

Mary giggles at my angst before answering, "Yes and no."

"Not very reassuring."

"Is meeting the parents supposed to be?" she smirks.

"No," I reply. "A necessary evil, I guess."

Mary transitions to a less playful demeanor as she reaches over to touch my arm while saying, "They'll love you, because I love you." Mary hesitates, trying to elicit some reassurance from me that I appreciated that fact before continuing, "You're the one for me.

I've known that from the start. Mother understands. Daddy will...at least in time."

"Does your dad have a gun?" I huff.

"Many," Mary quickly replies. "But, don't worry. He's only shot at one," she hesitates for a second to exaggerate, "maybe two of my boyfriends in the past."

"Hope he hit them," I jest.

Mary laughs, "I don't remember. I guess they didn't mean that much to me."

"That's good," I grin. "What are they like? Your parents, I mean. You've told me a little about them...but really not that much. I know your dad's a doctor and your mom likes to bake, but what are the really like?"

Mary hesitates as if calculating how much to tell before saying, "Mother is sweet...maybe a little naive, but in a good way. She believes almost everything and thinks the best about everyone. Daddy...well Daddy is the yin to her yang. He's more skeptical and pragmatic. He will test you, because that's his way, but don't worry."

"Why?" I nervously mutter.

Mary smiles, "Because you're with me, and I know how to— maneuver Daddy to my way of thinking."

"What should I call him?" I ask.

"You could try Daddy," Mary quips.

"I don't think so," I sigh.

"Daddy wouldn't get the humor either," she smiles. "His friends call him Robert."

"I doubt I qualify as a friend," I note.

Mary laughs, "Probably not—but I hope in time you'll be friends. How about you try Dr. McAnally?"

"I'll try," I mutter.

Mary's parents lived a few miles outside of Tahlequah. The roads became narrow and winding. The night is dark, and it seems as if we are heading nowhere. In the distance, a single light shines through the thick woods.

"That's it!" Mary exclaims. "Take the next drive to the left, and the house is up the hill."

The neatly graded rock drive leads to a large two-story house with stately columns defining the front porch. Even in the dim moonlight, I could tell the grand house is painted white. I knew Mary's father was a physician, but looking at this place, I realize he must be an extremely successful one. Mary bounds from the car almost before it completely stops. The front door opens at almost the same time. A tall, thin man wraps his arms around his daughter while her mother squeezes into the hug. Mary's parents look like shadows in the dark, but it's obvious they're glad to see her.

I'm slow to exit the car during their reunion before taking an inordinately long time to fumble with the bags in the trunk.

"You can't hide out forever," Mary whispers from behind me.

"I'm just getting our stuff," I explain.

"Sure," Mary smiles. "Let me help."

In a few seconds, I'm standing in the front room of this impressive home with Mary's parents inspecting me. Her mother smiles easily, and I expect at almost everyone. Her father, by contrast, studies my every move as if trying to determine how much scrutiny he'll put me through. By his disapproving body language, I anticipate a thorough examination. The next hour is a series of uncomfortable exchanges. Mary and her mother continually trying to cover for my clumsy responses to the even more awkward interrogation her father employs.

After a while, Mary's father tires of my disappointing answers to his inquisition and leaves the room. Mary's mother excuses herself to prepare my room, which I'm told will be in the attic loft. I assume my accommodation will be far from Mary's room, and I'm expecting a sturdy lock on the door.

"That wasn't too bad now, was it?" Mary whispers, after we are alone in the living room.

"Compared to waterboarding, no," I quip. "Although—I was wondering how bad waterboarding could be."

"Stop it," Mary banters. "Daddy's just interested in you."

"Interested in how to get rid of me," I whisper.

Mary smiles in her sweet way before saying, "Maybe—but hang in there. Mom likes you. That's something."

"What's this?" I ask, as I spy a unique feature in the tastefully decorated room.

A scale model of the RMS Titanic rests prominently on a credenza in the corner of the room. Being a long-time aficionado of all things Titanic, I move to take a closer look.

"Daddy's shrine," Mary answers.

"To the Titanic?"

Mary nods.

I continue to study the small but important display as I ask, "Why didn't you tell me? You know I'm into everything Titanic."

"I know you like watching those documentaries about the ship, but frankly, you never seem too interested in me talking about Daddy."

"That's fair," I grimace. "This model is incredibly detailed. It must have set him back a few bucks?"

"About $5,000," Mary confesses. "Mother didn't mind, but she did hate giving up this corner."

A couple of books about the tragic ship rest next to the model. One of them I recognize as a book I once checked out from the library. What I spy next nearly causes me to gasp.

"Is this—" I begin to ask before Mary's father interrupts from behind me.

"It's a copy of a steerage ticket to Titanic," Robert McAnally announces from behind my shoulder.

I quickly and carefully put the frame holding the ticket back on the credenza before facing Mary's father. He doesn't say anything at first, but walks next to me and picks up the frame and hands it back to me.

"The one on top is an actual ticket from Titanic," Dr. McAnally states, with a tone of justified satisfaction. "It's faded badly, so the one below is a facsimile of the authentic one." Dr. McAnally hesitates before adding, "Mary's told me you're quite a fanatic about Titanic."

"I don't know if I would say a 'fanatic,'" I defend. "I certainly don't have a collection like this. Obviously, you're a collector. Do you mind me asking where you found a ticket from Titanic?"

Dr. McAnally manages to contain his smile, although he seems pleased in the interest about his collection. He reaches for a picture hanging on the wall behind the credenza as he says, "It was hers." Dr. McAnally hands me an old photograph of a young woman who is obviously an ancestor of my Mary. "This is Maria Kelly. She was my grandmother and Mary's great-grandmother. She came to

America from Limerick, Ireland on the Titanic and somehow survived. She lost everything but the clothes on her back and what was in her pockets—including this ticket."

"That's unbelievable," I state. "I've always had an interest in Titanic, but to talk to someone who actually knew a survivor. I never expected that."

"My grandmother was very spry and determined," Dr. McAnally boasts. "I grew up hearing her story. I guess, I'm a fanatic, too."

"How old was she?" I ask. "When your grandmother made the trip, I mean."

"She was eighteen," Dr. McAnally informs. "She died in 1982 at 88 years old. She used to count the years that she had beat Titanic."

"Beat Titanic?" I quiz.

Dr. McAnally smiles, "She used to brag on every one of her birthdays that she had beat Titanic again, meaning she should have died, but instead she "beat" Titanic for seventy years after that night."

"I would have loved to have met her," I say, without thinking.

Dr. McAnally looks at me oddly before saying, "I would like to see her again myself. I believe you would have enjoyed meeting her."

Mary interrupts our conversation saying, "I'm tired, and I think my two men can talk more about Titanic in the morning. I'm ready to snuggle in my bed and listen for the storms. You want me to show Jeff to his room?"

"No," Dr. McAnally abruptly replies. "I'll show him to the loft."

Mary smirks mischievously, "I thought as much." She kisses me on the lips in front of her father. "See you in the morning," she whispers. As she walks away, and as a way to tease her father, she adds, "If not before."

"Well, then," Dr. McAnally huffs. "Let's get you stowed away."

I follow Dr. McAnally up the stairs to what I assume will be a bedroom on the second floor. Instead, he continues to a spiral staircase leading up an additional floor. I follow, and I'm soon standing in a small bedroom that has a single bed with an old trunk at the foot, a chest of drawers, a secretary desk, and a severely sloped ceiling.

"It's cozy," Dr. McAnally announces. "It's quiet up here. You should sleep well."

I nod. After an awkward moment of silence, I ask, "Did you know your grandmother well?"

Dr. McAnally smiles, "Very."

"I'd really like to ask you some questions about her memories of Titanic," I continue.

Before I can plead more, Dr. McAnally interrupts, "Tomorrow will be a good day for that."

"Of course," I concede.

Dr. McAnally looks frustrated with himself for using such a gruff tone, and says, with a more civil inflection, "This is one of my favorite rooms. I retreat from the downstairs chatter here. I work at this desk sometimes and can attest that this bed is comfortable for an afternoon nap. There is one downside, however."

"What's that?" I nervously inquire.

"You'll have to navigate the stairs to find the bathroom," he explains. "It's the second door on the right."

I look around a moment before quipping, "The door won't be locked from the outside?"

A slight laugh sneaks out of the doctor at my candor as he says, "I trust my daughter. I guess I'll learn to trust you. Sleep well."

Without further dialogue, Dr. McAnally leaves me in the isolated room. I go through my routine to prepare for bed, including another trip down the spiral staircase to kiss Mary goodnight. Once back in the room, I pull on a tattered pair of red sweatpants and bright yellow Oklahoma City Memorial Marathon tee shirt I received as part of a relay team from the previous year. I explore the small space. There is a single window looking out to the backyard. I put my things away. Before crawling into bed, I try the drop-down lid to the secretary desk. It's locked so I have no temptation to meddle. I put in the earphones to my iPod and doze off to the sound track of the movie Titanic. For some reason it seems appropriate, and I don't find many opportunities to listen to this part of my playlist. I have to carefully tilt my head between two ceiling joists to find my pillow. I slip the iPod into the pocket of my sweatpants, nestle my head into the soft pillow and stare at the bare wood ceiling only a few feet from my forehead for about half of the instrumental "*Southampton*" before falling into a deep sleep.

I don't know the time when a muffled grating sound of metal causes me to almost awaken. I fall back to sleep for a time before another sound startles me to full consciousness. I don't know the source of the frightful sound, but I quickly rise up smashing my head into the low ceiling. I let out a groan before reaching up to rub my head. I feel no bump and no blood, so I determine I'm uninjured.

The noise outside persists, however, and it takes me a moment to realize the illogic of the commotion. The sound comes from right outside my door and it appears, in my still drowsy state, to be a large number of people rushing about. That makes no sense as I wake up more and remember I'm in a small attic room with nothing but a narrow staircase outside my door. The uproar continues, however. I maneuver from under the low ceiling and feel the cold floor on my bare feet. I cautiously move toward the door before realizing how disoriented I've become. Nothing in the room seems the same as the night before. I pull the iPod out of my sweatpants and see it is nearly midnight. My room no longer has a single bed, but two sets of bunk beds.

"What's going on?" a strange voice in a thick Irish accent asks from the dark.

"Huh?" I groan.

"The racket outside," the voice clarifies.

"Do I know you?" I stammer.

"Only a day," the man says.

"What's going on?" another voice in a different accent asks.

"Don't know," the Irish voice replies.

"Let's see what the riot's about," yet a fourth voice demands.

Someone turns on an electric light as I nearly stumble to the floor. I am no longer in the comfortable loft of my girlfriend's parent's home, but in a strange place I only vaguely recognize. The small room has two sets of bunks on each side with a sink in between.

"What's up with him?" one of the strangers asks.

The Irish man looks at me a moment before saying, "I don't know. He's a strange one. Let's see what's up at this hour."

In a few minutes, the three strangers leave me alone. I sit on the edge of the bottom bunk and rub my head to try to clear my thoughts. What seems real cannot be real. I examine the room one more time. I've seen it in pictures, but it cannot be possible I am here. I'm sitting in a third-class cabin on Titanic.

I stumble outside to a scene of mass confusion, as people in all states of dress clamor in a long hallway. Their conversations are confused, and I cannot make any sense of the roaring noise. A young boy sprints by, and I reach out to catch his arm.

"What's going on?" I ask.

The boy looks at my strange clothes before replying, "I don't know, but I think the ship has hit something."

"What is this ship?" I demand, without letting go of his arm.

The boy looks strangely at me before saying, "Titanic."

I nod before asking, "What day is it?"

"Sunday, sir," the boy replies. "No—it's past midnight. It's Monday."

"What time is it?" I demand.

"I don't know" the boy says, as he squirms. "I don't have a watch, but it must be past midnight."

How can this be real? I'm standing in lower decks of Titanic dressed in my sweatpants and bright yellow tee shirt. This must be a dream, I think to myself. The crowd moves away from the area, and there is a moment of peace.

I'm dreaming, I think to myself again. It seems so real, but dreams are strange that way. A calm comes over me as I realize this cannot be real. I've always been mesmerized with the sinking of the Titanic and now my mind is letting me play the ultimate reality game. I've always wanted to be brave. This is my chance.

I move down the hall in the opposite direction the mob had traveled a few moments ago. The hallway is now silent and peaceful. My dream is very real, and I can feel myself moving slightly downhill. At the corner, a sign indicates I'm on "E" deck of Titanic.

From behind me, a female voice in a heavy Irish accent says, "Will the ship be stayin' afloat?"

I turn around to see my Mary standing in a simple white nightgown. I'm so surprised to see her that I cannot speak for a moment. She seems equally shocked to see me and carefully examines my sleep clothes.

"Are you part of the crew?" she asks warily. "Why are you wearing such odd clothes?"

"No, Mary," I smile. "I'm not part of the crew."

"Who's this Mary?" the woman asks.

"You."

"I'm not Mary," she corrects. "My name is Maria."

"Maria Kelly," I remember. "You're coming to America from Limerick—in Ireland."

"How would you know that, sir?" Maria demands.

I try to think of a way to explain how I know the great-grandmother of my girlfriend without spoiling the dream.

"I overheard someone," I lie.

"You've been spying on me?" she charges.

"No," I try to defend. "I'm—I'm here to help you."

Maria Kelly examines me carefully to determine if I might be trustworthy before saying, "Good then. Help me. I've been trying to get to the upper decks, but all the exits seem blocked either by people or gates. I was hoping you were part of the crew and could show me the way. "

"Of course," I say, as I try to think back to all the articles I've read and deck plans I've seen about the great ship. "Where are we?"

Maria fumes, "If you're going to help me, I would expect you to know that!"

"Calm down," I say. "I will help you. Trust me."

"And why should I trust a man I only just met?" she asks. "Especially one dressed in an unearthly yellow shirt?"

I nod, "I know it seems that way, but I am someone you can trust. Now, where are we?"

"E deck," Maria finally answers.

"Port or starboard," I ask.

"What?"

I sigh, "When facing the front of the ship, are we on the left or right side."

"Left."

"Are we closer to the front or the back of the ship?" I continue.

"Front."

I think for a moment before saying, "We need to get you up top and into a life boat."

Maria Kelly looks at me suspiciously, "The Titanic is unsinkable. Why on earth would I want to be in a lifeboat?"

"The Titanic is very sinkable," I state. "In fact, this boat will be under the sea in about two hours."

"I don't believe you," Maria replies.

"You don't have to, but it's the truth," I try to assure.

"Who are you?" Maria asks, with a quizzical tilt of her head.

"I'm Jeff Westbrook," I introduce.

"American?"

"Yes."

"Why are you dressed that way?"

I look down at my worn-out sweatpants and say, "I like to be warm when I sleep."

"You sleep in those?"

I nod.

"Put on a life vest," Maria demands. "I do not believe we are sinking, but please cover up that shirt."

I duck into the cabin and quickly locate one of the canvas life vests issued to all passengers.

Maria studies me a moment before saying, "So, Jeff Westbrook, if this boat is sinking, what should we do?"

"Like I said, we have to get you to the boat deck," I answer.

"Impossible," Maria bluntly states.

"Not impossible," I reply.

"I've been trying for nearly an hour to make my way up, but we're trapped," she assesses.

I listen to what this young woman has to say, determined not to argue with her. Her statement indicating she had been trying to move up from the lower deck for nearly an hour, almost fails to register with me.

"You've been up an hour?" I question.

"Yes," she sighs. "I woke up sometime after midnight."

"What time is it?" I ask.

"I don't know exactly," she replies. "The last clock I saw said it was 12:30. We heard rumors the ship was in trouble and even heard they were putting some passengers in the lifeboats, but suspect that was to make the first-class more at ease."

"Are you telling me it's later than 12:30?"

"I imagine it's closer to 1:15," Maria informs. "The deck keeps tilting more. I saw one of the Black Gang running through saying the water was a rising."

"Stay here," I command.

This dream seems too real, and the chaos has my adrenalin pumping. I make my way down the hall toward the front of the doomed ship. The deck becomes empty and eerily silent. I turn a corner to see a fearful sight as water stands almost a foot deep with personal items floating in the otherwise clear water. I wade into the icy water trying to find the forward stairwell, but the water stings my feet and they soon become numb. I retreat to find Maria.

Maria sees my sweatpants wet to my knees and can probably sense some panic in my face as she says, "We're sinking, aren't we Mr. Westbrook."

"Yes," I answer stoically. I think for moment before saying, "I need to know exactly what time it is."

I suddenly remember the iPod in my sweat pants, and I quickly reach into the pocket and look at the device. It reads 1:20 AM, April 15. It should say 2002, but by all of my observations the past few minutes, it is 1912. The battery is almost exhausted, but the time shows 1:20 AM.

"That's bad," I mutter.

"What is that?" Maria asks.

"It's already 1:20," I answer. "Half the lifeboats have already been launched. The chances of a third-class passenger making it to the deck before the last one leaves seems hopeless."

"That is bad," Maria confirms, "but I was asking about that thing in your hand."

I look down to see I'm still holding my iPod. "It's a music player," I inform.

"A what?"

I take the earplug and give it to her before hitting the button to play. She seems shocked at first, but then listens in amazement for a few seconds.

"Very nice," Maria smiles, "but why did it stop."

I take the device from her to see the battery has completely died.

"The batteries are dead," I say. "So are we if we don't get to the top."

For the next fifteen minutes, we frantically search for a way up. All of the stairwells are either blocked by masses of panicked people or completely shut off from above. This chaotic disaster has stranded hundreds of people. I can hear and feel their panic, but I know they have no idea they are doomed. This is a dream; I keep reminding myself. I can't save everyone, but maybe my mission is to save Maria Kelly.

"It's no use," Maria finally concedes. "We're not getting off this ship."

Her observation is pragmatic. The great ship continues to tilt downward and to the right. We tried and failed to find a way up. I've watched every documentary I could ever find and read countless articles about the great tragedy. I've gone over this exercise in my mind about how someone could survive. The glaring fact, however, is that no one survived the Titanic without getting on one of those lifeboats.

"Collapsible B," I whisper, almost to myself.

"What?"

I think a moment before answering her. "Collapsible B washes off the boat deck just a few minutes before the ship breaks apart. It was flipped over and floats off empty."

"That doesn't seem like a help," Maria frowns.

"It will be our only chance," I say grimily. "It floats off on the port side, but it's made out of cork. We've got to find a way to swim to Collapsible B. It's our only chance."

"If you say so," Maria sighs.

"Do you trust me?" I ask.

Maria looks at me strangely before saying, "I shouldn't. I mean, we've only just met, and you are as odd a fellow as I've ever run across. But—there's something in your eyes I like. I do trust you, Jeff Westbrook, but heaven knows why I should."

"Good," I smile. "We've only got a short amount of time, and timing is everything. We need to find a way to G deck."

"G deck?" Maria replies, with some alarm. "You asked me to trust you, but that's going the wrong way! Most of that deck must be underwater by now."

"Toward the bow of the ship, yes," I explain. "But back by the stern, where we're headed, it's high and dry. We need to find the pantry."

"I'm not hungry," Maria protests.

"Just trust me," I say.

We push our way against the hoard of frightened people trying desperately to escape to the decks above. I grab Maria's hand and pull her upwards toward the stern of the boat. We find a stairway heading down a few hundred feet after passing the steerage gangway to the ship. Titanic is calmer here and so quiet we can begin to hear the strain of metal as the ship continues to dip further into the icy ocean. We find F deck almost empty as I continue to drag Maria further into the lower decks of the ship.

G deck is close to the heart of the ship, where the work of the churning engines and the preparation of the massive amount of food for the thousands of people on board happen. My plan is thwarted, however, when I find we are blocked from the pantry area by a steel wall. We retreat to F deck and find a single small staircase that takes us to the panty on G deck.

"We don't have much time," I urgently inform, as I survey the large area of food stores.

"What are we looking for?" Maria quizzes.

"We need two empty milk cans, some rope, and lots of lard," I say. When I perceive her confusion, I add, "I told you to trust me."

"I'm trying," she moans.

I quickly find two large milk cans standing about three feet high. I frown when they are full of milk. Without hesitation, I pour the milk out on the floor, while Maria looks on in disbelief. Once empty, I immediately reseal the empty cans.

"I'll need that," I say, as I spy a simple wooden bench one of the workers used to peel potatoes.

"You're making a raft," Maria surmises.

"A very temporary one," I assure.

I take out my iPod to check the time before realizing it is out of battery. I see Maria looking at the strange device. I hand it to her and say, "Here's a souvenir of our adventure."

Maria smiles and puts the iPod in her pocket.

"We need to do one more thing," I say timidly.

"What's that?" Maria asks.

As I pull down a heavy container of lard, I say, "We need to cover ourselves in this."

"Excuse me!" Maria protests. "Whatever makes you think a good girl like me would ever do such a thing?"

I sigh deeply before explaining, "The water out there is freezing. We won't last a minute in it if we were to fall off this makeshift raft. We have to get off this ship and into the water a few minutes before the ship breaks in two. Collapsible B will be there off the port side, but we'll be in the water long enough that hypothermia will kill us if we fall into the ocean. A thick coating of lard from head to toe will insulate us—at least for a short time and might keep the cold water off our skin long enough to make a difference."

Mary grimaces, "You make it mighty hard for a girl to trust you, Jeff Westbrook. I'll do it, but not in front of you!"

"Of course," I reply, as I hand her a large container of the lard. "I'll go to the other room. Put the lard on thick as you can and put all your clothes back on afterward. Call when you're ready."

I retire to another room and slather the lard all over my body before putting my sweatpants and shirt back on. It's only about two minutes before I hear Maria say, "I'm decent."

She is a mess, and I quickly realize I must look equally ridiculous.

"I begin to see your plan, Mr. Westbrook," Maria says, with as much dignity as she can muster. "But I do have one question."

"Yes."

"To get this raft of yours into the water and float to this boat that you say will be there, we will need to get to the boat deck. I've already failed to find a way and even with your help we've been blocked."

I reply, "The gangplank door on the port side was—is opened on F about mid-deck. It might be a slight drop to the water, but we should be able to make it." I think for a moment. "I wish I knew the exact time."

"It's a little past 2 AM," Maria announces.

"You know that for sure?" I question.

"I think so," Maria replies. "I dropped that little thing you gave me and it flashed 2 AM just before I called for you. It—it went off again, unfortunately."

"We don't have much time," I say. "We have to move!"

I drag one milk can and the small bench while Maria manages to bring the other milk can. We move forward on F deck and the slope is much steeper now. As I had seen in one of my documentaries about this night, the gangplank door on F deck is open. The water is already close to the door, which is frightful, but means we will not have a long drop to the water. It also indicates this ship is about to burst in two. I lay the two milk containers side by side and put the wooden bench on top of them. I managed to find a short piece of string to lash them together and even use the wire of my earplugs to secure one of the lids to the milk cans.

Maria is calmer than I would have imagined, but the water is rising fast now. I tug at her lifejacket and make sure it's secure. She's a mess with her face covered in lard, but there's something about her that reminds me how much I love my Mary.

"These cans will barely keep us out of the water," I explain. "We'll need to paddle as far as we can from the ship and look for the capsized boat."

Maria nods.

"Maria," I continue. "It's going to be cold and miserable out there. You're going to see terrible things tonight. Many will perish. Don't give up. A ship is on its way. When this ship goes down, it will be two or three hours before the rescue ship arrives. Never give up."

"I don't know how you know these things," Maria shakes, as the cold outside air blows against us. "I do trust you. I have the feeling you know what is going to happen. Are you a prophet—or maybe my angel?"

"I'm no angel," I confess. "I'm—you'll find this hard to believe, but I'm in love with your great granddaughter. I'm not from this place—or this time. I know this sounds crazy, but I think this is all a big adventurous dream. I'm from a place called Oklahoma. I know you make it safe because your family lives there now."

"Oklahoma," Maria smiles. "I don't know the place, but I like the sound of the name. You're right. I do think you might be a little touched, but you have helped me. I believe you have saved me, and I will never forget that."

"We need to cast off," I say.

I pull the small raft made of large milk cans to the still water. I take Maria by the hand and make sure she is squarely placed. The small raft sinks lower than I thought, and there will not be enough room for me.

When Maria is safely on the raft I say, "I'm going to give you a push. Brace yourself. I'll jump and hang on until we find Collapsible B."

"You'll freeze," Maria insists.

"I'll be fine," I assure. "I'm a strong swimmer, and this lard has to help keep some of the cold off."

I cautiously give Maria a push away from Titanic. The water is like a mirror, and the stars shine brilliantly above on this moonless night. Maria looks brave and sure on our little raft. I jump and feel a searing pain as my head hits the top of the gang plank door. I hear Maria scream, and my body hits the icy water. I feel myself being pulled helplessly into the dark abyss. Maria's screams are muffled as I sink deeper into the water. I'm panicked, terrified, and fighting for my life as I slowly sink away. It's only a dream, I think to myself. This can't be real. Wake up!

I wake up with water pouring off my face. It takes me a moment to realize my face is all that's wet. I'm dry and safe in the bed in the loft of the McAnally home.

"He's awake!" I hear a concerned Mary shout.

A painful beam of light shines in my eyes and the intimidating Dr. McAnally stands over me.

"He'll be fine," Dr. McAnally announces, with a veiled hint of disappointment.

"What—happened?" I ask.

"You bumped your head," Mary says. "I told Daddy it was ridiculous to put you up here. This old ceiling is so low by the bed. You must have tried to get up in the night and hit your head. When you didn't come down, I came to check on you."

"What time is it?" I ask.

"Almost nine," Dr. McAnally interrupts.

I whisper to myself, "She would be on Carpathia by now—safe."

"What did you say?" Dr. McAnally demands.

"Oh—nothing," I reply. "I had a dream. It was so real. I was on Titanic. I was there right to the moment it broke apart."

"The mind will take you to strange places," Dr. McAnally reasons.

"Is he going to be okay, Daddy?" Mary pleads.

Dr. McAnally looks at me strangely before saying, "He'll be fine. I'll take him to the hospital when he dresses, and we'll do an MRI just so you won't worry. We'll keep an eye on him to see if he has any symptoms. My guess is that he knocked himself out then fell asleep. He'll be fine."

Mary sits on the bed by my side and asks softly, "What was it like?"

I'm still not fully awake and mutter, "What?"

Mary puts her hand on my shoulder and coaxes, "Titanic. What was it like? What was she like?"

I look over at Dr. McAnally expecting him to be confused or disapproving, but instead he seems to nod at me to share my dream.

"I don't remember telling you," I answer. "I did have a dream—a vivid dream—so vivid it seemed real." I hesitate a moment before saying, "I don't remember telling you about my dream when I woke up. I must still be groggy. What did I say before?"

"Nothing," Mary responds, almost cheerfully.

"Then how did you know?" I ask woozily.

Mary glances at her father before explaining, "Gi Gi—my great grandmother Maria—told me when I was a little girl. When she died I was only eight, but old enough to remember the story."

"Mary, I had a dream," I protest. "Albeit a very lucid and memorable one. You can't think I actually—went back in time to meet your great grandmother. Surely you agree, Dr. McAnally."

Mary's father does not respond, and Mary quickly interrupts, "Daddy knows the story better than me. He heard the stories for years before I was even born."

"It's impossible," I reply.

Mary thinks for a moment before saying, "You've told me nothing of your dream?"

"Not that I remember," I admit. "I was knocked out, so I don't know what I might have said."

"You've said nothing," Mary assures. "But I know what you've been through tonight. You woke up in third-class dazed and confused. You found my great grandmother lost and alone in the lower decks of Titanic. You tried to convince her this was impossible, just like you're doing with me. You led her through the lower decks of Titanic, helped her build a small raft, and told her about the Collapsible B lifeboat that saved her life. She told me these stories when I was a girl and said I would meet the man who saved her. His name would be Jeff Westbrook, and now you're here!"

"That could be a coincidence," I reply. "Jeff Westbrook's not the most unusual name in the world. Your story does sound a lot like my dream, but—maybe I've heard you tell the story."

"I've never told you anything about my Gi Gi," Mary interjects. "I purposely have avoided talking to you at all about my family's journey to America."

"Maybe I read about your great grandmother's story in an article," I argue, "or maybe I saw her story in a documentary sometime and it stuck in my subconscious."

"Gi Gi said her Jeff Westbrook wore colorful cloths," Mary argues. "Specifically, some kind of red pants, that later in her life she knew were sweatpants, and a bright yellow shirt with a blue tree on it." Mary pauses, "A shirt that said Oklahoma City Memorial Marathon. A shirt like you're wearing right now and a description of your grungy old sweatpants. She met you, Jeff. I don't know how, and I don't know why, but I know it happened."

Dr. McAnally finally interrupts, "Jeff's had a blow to the head. Maybe we should let him rest. Go downstairs, Mary. We'll take Jeff for his MRI when he makes it down."

Mary looks like she might argue, but instead heads down the spiral stairs leaving her father and me alone.

"I've never seen Mary so adamant," I say, once she is gone. "It's not her nature. What do you think happened? I probably heard about your grandmother's survival story, and something clicked that caused me to dream. Everything else was coincidence. Right?"

Dr. McAnally stares at me a moment before saying, "I never thought anyone good enough for my Mary. I heard my grandmother's Titanic story since I was a child. I can't say I ever believed in it like Mary. When she met a man named Jeff Westbrook, I was suspicious. Stories told to a young girl by an old woman could have had an effect on her choice of a companion.

I'll not deny I've purposefully avoided you and waited until tonight to make up my mind."

"And?"

Dr. McAnally thinks for a moment before responding. "Grandma Maria—that's what I always called her—said your guidance through the lower deck, thinking of building a raft, and knowing the exact time to push her out that gangplank door saved her life. She also informed me many times that covering herself in lard had no good effect and nearly caused her to slip off the capsized boat until it washed off her feet."

"You can't believe I was there?" I protest.

"Logic tells me no," Dr. McAnally shrugs. "Facts, however strange, are hard things to ignore. Tell me, have you seen your iPod this morning?"

I check my pocket, but discover the device is missing. I quickly look under the pillow and around the sides of the bed to no avail.

I finally look at Dr. McAnally and say, "I've lost it."

"You gave it to my grandmother," he corrects.

"How could you know that detail?" I inquire.

Dr. McAnally smiles strangely as he steps to the secretary desk in the corner of the room. He slowly removes a small key from his pocket and unlocks the lid to the desk.

"I normally have this with the other artifacts," Dr. McAnally explains. "When I invited you here, I had to know, so I locked it away. Grandmother did not know what it was for many years. In the 60s, I believed it to have something to do with the Beatles with the Apple logo and all. My family did well by investing in the Apple Company. Maria slid off the collapsible before she was able to secure herself, and the sea water didn't do it much good, but it was my grandmother's favorite possession."

When Dr. McAnally turns around, he hands me a corroded and discolored iPod. I gasp when I see my initials etched on the back cover.

Dr. McAnally has a strained smile as he says, "My grandmother predicted this would happen. She would want me to say, 'Welcome to the family, Jeff Westbrook.'"

THE END

THE BOOK COVER

The first day of school bristled with anticipation of a new year and the regret of a summer gone. Early September's heat and humidity in southeast Texas made it seem as if summer should continue endlessly. The board of education, the calendar, and the parents, however, said it was time for school.

Keith didn't mind. Any angst about the lost freedom of summer was tempered by the fact he secretly liked school. He looked forward to seeing his friends together again, the structure of the school rules, the challenges, and the familiar smells of the building, like the lunch ladies cooking cinnamon rolls. Keith could hold his own on the football field or the basketball court but math, English, and social studies were where he excelled. He would have Mrs. Dewalt this year. Former students said she was tough, but kids from her class had won the school-wide science fair two years in a row. Fourth grade was going to be a great year. Keith was sure of that.

Mrs. Dewalt had her teacher-face glaring the minute Keith entered the classroom. She stood tall with dark, flashing eyes that seemed to interrogate each student. Her hair was straight and curled up at her shoulders. She was somewhat soft-spoken, but her demeanor left no doubt she would not be tested. What stood out most to Keith were her brightly painted red fingernails that always seemed immaculate. Mrs. Dewalt was younger than some teachers, but she had been around enough to know how to handle rowdy boys. Her desks were aligned with precision, indicating high expectations. Any horseplay would not be tolerated. Textbooks stacked neatly in the corner and the tattered SRA® reading laboratory added to the sense of order. Learning was important at Washington Elementary—at least in Mrs. Dewalt's class.

The students sat in quiet anticipation as their teacher surveyed her class. It seemed like minutes, but was possibly only a few seconds, before Mrs. Dewalt gave measured and specific instructions for each student to move in an orderly fashion to the corner and take their assigned reading and math books from the stack. Mrs. Dewalt then handed out sheets of thick construction paper to the class. She took the opportunity to give a heartfelt lecture about the responsibly each student had to take good care of the books.

"You have an obligation to treat your books with respect," Mrs. Dewalt would say. "Books will give you the knowledge to expand your horizons and create your own best future."

Erman Russell and Michael Bruno dared to whisper during Mrs. Dewalt's lecture. She walked behind Erman and grabbed him by the ear to say, "Are you listening to me?"

Keith covered his mouth with his hand to muffle his laughter. Others were not so disciplined, and the riotous giggles cost the class their first recess of the school year. Erman was often in trouble and had difficulty sitting still for any length of time. Michael was the chatterbox of the class and did not know how to keep his mouth shut at the appropriate time. They were both friends of Keith, but spent significantly more time after school for their mischiefs than he.

Mrs. Dewalt was deliberate as she instructed, "Take the paper and make a line, now half the line. Fold the first flap over and be careful. You only have the book covers I've given you. If you do not follow directions, or if you are careless, you will have a crooked cover for the rest of the year."

Keith followed the directives as if his entire school career depended on it. The reading book had worn corners and a binding that had been re-glued. Several names were printed in the front cover identifying students who owned the book in previous years. The math book was in slightly better shape, but still faded. Keith was proud of his cover. He had folded the paper as instructed, cut carefully, and pasted neatly. If not for Kathleen Welch, his would have been one of the best. Kathleen's father was a doctor, and she had always been one of the brightest girls in his class. The girls always seemed better at cutting book covers, but Keith didn't mind. In fact, Kathleen was not only neat in her work, but she was also the prettiest girl in class. Keith smiled broadly when he caught her checking out his book cover.

The lessons went quickly on the first day, and by the afternoon, Keith moved to the back corner to use the SRA® reading lab. He had worked his way through purple, red, and orange last year and was sure he would reach the gold, brown, and tan in a few weeks, if he would apply himself. Kathleen Welch already read the gold stories, but Keith had a goal of getting to the lime section in the reading lab before her.

It was a hot afternoon when class dismissed. Keith believed he could handle Mrs. Dewalt's rigor, and felt he had a very good first day. Erman and Michael had already caught Mrs. Dewalt's wrath and were beating erasers on the sidewalk as Keith started his walk home. His other friend Russell had made the mistake of pushing a girl on the playground, and he was sent to the principal's office. The class hadn't seen him since, but expected the worst.

The pecking order at Washington Elementary meant any older grade could "report" a lower grade to any teacher. That usually involved swats from the teacher. A teacher sending a student to the principal was a much more serious offense. Mr. Young, the principal at Washington Elementary, possessed several different paddles depending on the offence. The regular paddle was what Keith believed would be used on Russell on the first day. Mr. Young also kept a paddle with electric tape wrapped around it to add to the pain. Another paddle had holes drilled in it to make an even firmer statement. It was rumored he kept a paddle with electric tape and holes drilled in it, and of course, Mr. Young kept an electric paddle for the most serious offenses. No one had ever seen the electric paddle. In fact, no student could actually say they had seen the electric tape and the paddle with the holes drilled in it, but everyone in the fourth grade knew they had to exist.

Keith didn't wait for his friends, as they received their after-school punishments. With his new reading and math books under his arm, he headed home to watch an episode of *Star Trek* and work on the day's homework assignment. Keith's dad worked at the Coca Cola® Bottling Company and wouldn't be home until nearly six o'clock. His mother had taken some work on the other side of town for some extra cash, now that all of her children were in school. For a few glorious minutes, Keith had the house to himself. The peaceful solitude did not last. Soon his younger brother arrived. His two older sisters showed up a little later, and with their constant babbling, they went directly to the girls' room without noticing Keith or his younger brother. Mom made it home close to five to begin supper. Keith's after school vacation was over for the day as Mom barked orders to finish the chores and start on homework before supper.

By the time Dad arrived, supper was on the table. Keith's two older brothers, Nathanial and James, were home by then. James was in high school and played football. Nathanial was a freshman in high school and surlier than the oldest brother. The conversation at the supper table was clearly one-way. Dad asked a few pointed questions about his children's behavior, while Mom focused more on the social happenings of the school day.

Keith's brothers and sisters had learned through the years less information they volunteered, the better. His mom, however, had spies everywhere and grilled him about the trouble Russell had found on the first day of school. Each of Keith's answers elicited stern looks from his two older brothers as they nonverbally were reinforcing the culture of giving the parents as little information as possible. After successfully surviving his mother's inquisition, Keith breathed a sigh of relief as his father added one parting warning to all of his children that punishment at school would trigger an equal to, if not greater, reckoning at home.

Keith had been victim to this firm rule last year when he was pushed into Mrs. Hurd's room after recess. He had done nothing wrong, but he was the one Mrs. Hurd had seen, and he got two swats for it. When he complained to his mother, she was sympathetic and even said she had a mind to go to the school and talk to Mrs. Hurd or Mr. Young about it. In the end, Keith got two swats on the behind from his mother and considered himself lucky she took care of it instead of turning it over to his father. His brother just older than him, Nathanial, had chided him for telling on himself. Nathanial was the more serious of his brothers. Keith could never tell if Nathanial was trying to be helpful or just determined to make his life miserable. He figured the truth was in the middle somewhere.

After supper, Keith looked over his new schoolbooks. He really didn't have an assignment for the first day, but he liked the feel of his new books and imagined what the year ahead might offer. He was too engrossed in his books to hear his brother Nathanial sneak up behind him. Without warning, Nathanial grabbed Keith's reading book and nearly caused Keith to tear the new cover he had put on that morning.

"Give it!" Keith demanded, although he had little leverage to make his older and bigger brother do anything.

Nathanial ignored his brother and casually thumbed through the book.

"Give it back!" Keith hissed. When his brother ignored him, Keith hears himself threaten, "Give it back or I'll—"

"You'll tell Mom," Nathanial interrupted. "I know, and I'm so scared."

Keith's only real threat to his older brothers seemed to be to inform them he would tell Mom, but that usually only meant they tormented him more.

"Come on," Keith pleaded. "Give it back before you tear it."

"Tear it!" Nathanial huffed. "Tear what? This paper cover Mrs. Dewalt had you glue on? You're pathetic!"

Nathanial tossed the book on the bed with a careless twisting motion. Keith desperately recovered his book and quickly inspected it for any accidental damage.

"You're a fool!" Nathanial chastised.

Keith countered, "The Bible says you're not supposed to call your brother a fool."

"I call it like I see," Nathanial retorted. "You're a fool to think that old book means anything."

"Mrs. Dewalt says books are knowledge," Keith argued. "She says books are opportunity."

"Maybe some books," Nathanial conceded. "But not this old thing."

"What's wrong with my book?" Keith challenged.

"Man," Nathanial sighed. "You're not only a fool, you're stupid too—or maybe blind. Let me see this thing."

Nathanial reached for the book in Keith's hand. At first Keith resisted, but his brother pulls gently and steadily until he has possession.

"Look at this," Nathanial said, as he opens up the front cover of the book revealing a list of names covering several school years. "Ten people had this book before you."

"So," Keith shrugs. "It's still a good book."

Nathanial shakes his head, "You don't get it. Look at these names. Brett, Molly, Emily, Dustin, Luke—Luke was the unlucky one. Then there's Gloria, Andre, Jalen, Reggie, and Terrance—and now you."

"So."

"So?" Nathanial mocked. "Luke was the last white kid to have this old book. See the Edison Elementary stamp? All of your books come from the white school after the white kids get something new. I feel bad for old Luke here. He nearly had a book as old as the ones in the black school. Don't you get it? You've got second-hand books at your second-hand school. That makes you a second-hand person."

Keith grabbed the book from his brother and carefully studied the names. He's right. Keith knew Terrance from the grade ahead and even knew who Reggie was, although Reggie was now a sixth-grader. The other names he did not know. He had looked at the list of names before and understood someone named Brett had this book brand new. Every year another student put their name on the book. He had not realized until this moment that he had never had a new book. He just took it for granted that all books were used. They all were at Washington Elementary.

"That's the old books from the white school," Nathanial explained. "When you get to high school, you'll know."

"I'm no second-hand person," Keith huffed. "Give me my book back!"

Nathanial smirks, as he says, "No problem. This old book don't mean anything more than you do."

Keith does not give his brother the satisfaction of responding to his insult but holds the book more loosely now. Keith is used to his older brother giving him a hard time about almost everything. Nathanial's stinging comment about his second-hand book planted a seed of doubt Keith had not previously considered. He knew Washington Elementary was a "black school." He understood his part of town—his community was segregated from the rest of the city. It had never bothered him before this night, however.

Keith's world had been safe. He understood his community. Kathleen Welch's father was the doctor—his doctor. Erman's dad worked at the refinery, as did much of the neighborhood. The store manager at the Ben Franklin Five & Dime was black. His teacher and preacher and every other adult he knew was black. Keith realized the other side of town was different. He knew the other schools were white. He knew his mother traveled to that part of town to do sewing and other odd jobs. Before now, Keith thought he understood his city. His brother Nathanial told him his book was second-hand, which inferred it was second-rate. He went to sleep in his safe bed, in his safe neighborhood, but had questions he had never considered.

The second day of school proved to be another hot September day in Texas. Keith's enthusiasm for school was not diminished, but he had a question, which had bothered him all night. He had wanted to ask his father, but thought that too intimidating. His mother might have an answer, but she was too busy to bother in the morning as she prepared for her day. Mrs. Dewalt would know, he thought to himself. She'll be able to answer my question.

Mrs. Dewalt did not give her students much time to think about the end of summer or allow the boys to get in more trouble from their mischief. It was the second day of school, and Mrs. Dewalt was determined to whip her new class into an efficient learning experience. Her intensity was intimidating. Mrs. Dewalt firmly understood strict discipline and demanding tasks would get the school year started her way—the way she knew would work. Keith wanted to ask his question all day, but never found the time. He waited until after school and would probably miss the first few minutes of *Star Trek*, but his question was important—at least it was to him.

"What is it?" Mrs. Dewalt sighs, with a weary tone when she sees Keith loitering around her desk.

"Can I ask you a question?" Keith stammers.

Mrs. Dewalt stares at him a moment before saying, "I think you just did." He looks sheepishly at his feet before Mrs. Dewalt says, "What's your question, Keith? I know it's important if you've stayed after school."

Keith nods, "It's about my book."

"Have you lost your book?" Mrs. Dewalt inquires, in an almost scolding tone.

"No—no," Keith defends. "I have it right here."

Keith quickly displays the book to prove he has his copy intact.

"What about your book?" Mrs. Dewalt asks, in a more consolatory tone. "Is there something wrong with it?"

Keith shakes his head and swallows hard before saying, "No ma'am. I put the book cover on like you said. I did my reading last night. It's just—it's just my brother—"

"Which one?" Mrs. Dewalt interjects.

"Nathanial," Keith responds.

"Of course," Mrs. Dewalt nods, in a way indicating she's not surprised. "What did Nathanial say?"

"Well," Keith begins, "he was showing me that this book has been used by ten different people. He said this is a ten-year-old book?"

"I doubt it's quite that old," Mrs. Dewalt replies, "but it is a book that's been used for a few years. Sometimes a student moves and a book is reassigned. I assure you this book still fits with our reading assignments for the year."

Keith nods, "It's just that Nathanial said this book came from the white school. He told me they always get the new books, and we get the hand-me-downs. He said this is a second-hand book." Keith hesitates before asking, "Am I a second-hand person?"

Mrs. Dewalt does not seem surprised by the question and appears to purposefully avoid any immediate reaction to her student's question. "Let me see your book," Mrs. Dewalt gently requests.

Keith hands over his book, and for a few moments, Mrs. Dewalt carefully examines it.

"I picked this book out for you, Keith," Mrs. Dewalt finally says. "It was in the best shape. Mrs. Hurd told me last year when she had you that you liked to read. I thought you should have one of the best books. You're right—but you're also wrong. These books were originally assigned to Edison Elementary. They used them for a few years before the books were sent here. You're right to think we sometimes receive second-hand books—and supplies, but that doesn't make this book any less special. Do you know what I like best about books?"

"No," Keith replies.

Mrs. Dewalt continues examining the book as she smiles, "Once words are in a book, they are there to last. I can read them and then pass them on to others. Words represent ideas—sometimes big ideas. It's not much of a book that gets read once and then discarded. I like when a book is well used—it gives it character, much like a person's experiences give them character." Mrs. Dewalt puts the book down to look at Keith before she continues, "You are not a second-hand person—unless you think of yourself that way. I'm a little disappointed Nathanial said something like that to you, but I had an older brother when I was younger and know they sometimes say things they don't really mean. You'll get out of this book what you put into it—whether it's old or new."

"What do you mean?" Keith asks.

"When you're reading, you're thinking. You're thinking about the way things are, or maybe you're dreaming of the way things could be. Either way, you're thinking, and thinking is good. These books can take you far, if you'll listen to them. I have high hopes and high expectations for my students. This book being second-hand doesn't make you second-class. There will be some that will want you to think that, but don't you let them—ever. Believe in yourself and be willing to work a little harder than the next guy, and you'll go far, Keith."

Keith nods and smiles faintly.

Mrs. Dewalt studies him before asking, "Do you think you'll beat Kathleen this year?"

"Beat her in what?" Keith confusingly asks.

"In the SRA® reading lab," Mrs. Dewalt clarifies. "She's one color ahead of you right now, but you—seem determined."

"I don't know," Keith meekly replies. "What do you think, Mrs. Dewalt? Can I beat her?"

Mrs. Dewalt smiles, "I believe you can, but that's not what's important."

"What's important then?"

"What's important is what you believe you can do," Mrs. Dewalt grins. "You can do anything you believe you can do—old book or not."

Keith smiles broadly and nods to acknowledge his teacher's encouragement.

"And Keith," Mrs. Dewalt adds, in a more serious tone. "You may have an old book, but that's a new book cover. I'll expect you to take good care of your book and return it at the end of the year in no worse shape than you received it."

"Yes, ma'am," Keith confirms, before cautiously leaving Mrs. Dewalt to her room to finish her long day.

Keith felt better after talking to Mrs. Dewalt. All the other kids had been right. Mrs. Dewalt was a tough and demanding teacher. She taught him many things that year, but none of her lessons would be as valuable as her private encouragement for him to believe in himself. Whenever he was faced with a problem that seemed impossible, Mrs. Dewalt would simply say, "There's always a way."

During the painful years of desegregation Keith would be tested in many ways, but the words a fourth-grade teacher on a September afternoon always gave him some strength to persevere. Mrs. Dewalt would say, "Define yourself, and the negative things others say about you will be irrelevant and ineffective as you make your way through life."

The challenges for Keith would continue through high school, in college, as a naval officer, and later in his business life. Keith would find many times when others tried to judge or label his worth, but he learned in the fourth grade from a teacher named Mrs. Dewalt that what others said meant little compared to how he thought about himself.

THE END

THE GENERATIONS

Golf laminated three generations of my family together in ways I did not completely appreciate when I was sixteen-years-old. My grandfather took up the game late in life. He grew up working hard on a cotton farm and hunted squirrels as much for food as sport. Like many of his generation, he migrated from the farm to town. He married well, began a business, and by age fifty, could be considered prosperous. He still liked to hunt quail and deer in season for sport, but a doctor recommended more exercise for his general health. Grandpa never considered golf as a source of leisure until then, but with a doctor's recommendation, he bought a set of clubs and became a golfer.

My grandfather's approach to the game was simple—find more golf balls than you lose. Over the years, he accumulated several decades of found balls in various states of playability. His two favorite clubs were his putter and ball dipper. By the time I was old enough to play with the adults, my grandfather was retired. At fourteen, I had the perfect life. Dad would drop me off at the golf course on his way to work. I would hit balls, putt, and play with friends until Dad showed up after work to play a round in the evening. I also played several times a week with Grandpa and the old men at the Elks Club. Grandpa swung with an efficient, yet unorthodox, arm swing. He carried a full arsenal of irons but rarely used any of them. Grandpa was deadly with his three-wood from 175 yards to 90 yards. Much closer than that, he would pull out the putter. He rarely hit the ball farther than 175 yards, but was almost never out of the fairway.

He tolerated sand traps. His hand lob, where he tossed the ball out of the sand, was an effective tool. Grandpa avoided water hazards at all cost. He played old water balls for any shot that might have to cross a wet hazard. I doubt Jack Nicklaus could have hit his old water balls more than 200 yards, but Grandpa was expert at directing shots over footbridges, even if they weren't on line with the hole he was playing. Grandpa's rules for water hazards were different from the Royal and Ancient's definition. He never hit more than one ball in the water before carrying it to the other side. Any ball hit in the water required him to fish at least two out with his ball dipper. By the time I played regularly with Grandpa and the old men, he spent at least ten minutes at every water hole whether he knocked one in or not. Ironically, Grandpa consistently complained about a player in another group as being "the worst ball hawk" at the club. Grandpa enjoyed the game, tolerated my youthful temper, and got his exercise.

My father had a passion for golf that far outpaced his abilities. One of my earliest childhood memories was watching Dad putt on the living room carpet during the nightly news. Dad practiced religiously, read all kinds of books on the golf swing, and tried to incorporate any article from *Golf Magazine* into his game. He never took a lesson but made up for his lack of instruction by sheer effort. Dad always had a curious loop in his swing, which produced a persistent and sometimes controllable slice. By the time I was a teenager, Dad could maneuver his chronic left to right ball movement and a scrappy wedge game to where he broke 80 more times than not.

For some reason, Dad struggled to incorporate into his own swing the techniques he studied in books and articles, but they came more naturally to me. Dad was my primary instructor and coach. I had an aptitude for the swing and hitting the shot that always eluded my father: I could hit a draw. I was a decent player that managed to play four years of high school golf and four years of college golf, even with two glaring flaws in my game. The first, and most frustrating, was my putting. I never had a good touch with the putter. My alignment and ability to read a green were nearly as bad. In one tournament during high school, I putted for thirteen birdies and one eagle without making one. I missed four greens all day and shot a four over par 76. That's some respectable ball striking and world-class lousy putting.

I had a deeper flaw in my game that proved more damaging and took more years to overcome—my temper. As long as I hit every shot perfectly, I was fine. Anyone who's played golf knows every round has less than perfect shots. There is such a thing as unconscious incompetence: when a person has a problem, but doesn't know it. I had what is known as conscious incompetence. I knew I had a terrible temper, and struggled to control it, but usually failed. I would write messages on my golf glove, try deep breathing exercises, and even have talks with myself—which generally turned into arguments with myself that I would lose.

With age came some maturity and eventually some control of my temper, but at age sixteen, I was a hopeless hothead. Both my father and grandfather endured it. Grandpa played the sport purely for exercise and did not understand how I could become so worked up over a game. Dad was a more competitive player, but he was always under control with his temper on and off the course. I ended up being the silly one, although that was hard for me to realize then.

Our favorite place to play golf was in the Sandhills of North Carolina at the Southern Pines Golf Club. We planned the trip all year, made the drive across country, and then played golf until we nearly dropped. Southern Pines was a Donald Ross classic that wasn't too long but was like walking through a golfing paradise over rolling hills and towering pine trees. The grass was green and the domed-shaped greens were hard and fast. My dad loved Southern Pines, although it punished his pronounced left-to-right shot. Grandpa was happy with any course that had shade and not too many carries across water. I always felt at home at Southern Pines and can still hear the sharp sound of a well-hit shot echoing through the pines.

It was next to the last day of our trip. We played an early round of golf, but on a perfect evening, we wanted to play a few holes more. Andy, the local pro, took a liking to my dad for some reason. He appreciated the distance we traveled to play his course and was always quick to accommodate us when he could. On this evening, he came out to the putting green, where Dad worked on mastering his Bullseye putter, and offered to let us play a quick nine before the sun went down. However, his boys were putting up the electric carts, and we would have to walk. I was used to walking during tournament play. Dad and Grandpa were prepared with their collapsible Bagboy aluminum pull carts.

My drive off the first hole that evening is one I still remember. I ripped a persimmon-headed driver that started perfectly down the right edge of the fairway, as it drew gently to the center, before catching the downhill slope. Dad cut his into the fairway about 70 yards behind me, while Grandpa pecked his tee shot right down the middle. We all put our second shots on the green and all made par. Of course, I missed a six-footer for birdie and celebrated by whacking my foot with the putter, which did no good, but relieved some stress.

The shadows were long, and it could not have been a more perfect day—well almost. By the fourth hole, Grandpa prepared for the water hazard we would face on the ninth hole. He dug through his bag with a steady and deliberate cadence. He continued for several minutes before Dad asked with a significant lack of patience, "What are you doing?"

Without looking up, my grandpa replied, "I'm looking for my ball dipper."

"I took it out," Dad informed.

"What?"

"I took it out before we left home," Dad answered. "We came to play golf, not hunt balls. You've got more balls than you could ever possibly lose, anyway."

Grandpa nodded his reluctant acceptance but continued to rattle through his bag while Dad tried to step up for his tee shot. Dad backed away three times, before saying, "Are you going to play golf or fiddle with your bag?"

Grandpa stopped his ruckus, but Dad, in his frustration, pulled his drive to the left side of the fairway. The second shot on the fourth hole went up a steep hill guarded on the left by a towering pine tree and two bunkers. Grandpa pecked his second shot about 40 yards short of the green. I was in good position of the right side of the fairway, so we stopped as Dad prepared for his difficult shot on the left side. The shot needed a slight right-to-left draw, but that shot had eluded my dad for his entire golfing career. Dad took a little extra time plotting his strategy to leave him the best chance to save a par.

As Dad wiggled and waggled in preparation for his shot, Grandpa, for some reason, decided to get a head start and crept slowly up the hill as Dad addressed the ball. Grandpa was out of sight and moving in a way he thought was silent. Unfortunately, his Bagboy pull cart needed some grease and the wheels made a distinctive, high pitch squeak. Grandpa could not hear it, but Dad sure did. Dad would stop addressing the ball to glare at Grandpa. Grandpa would stand still until Dad tried to set up to the ball again. As soon as Dad's back was turned, Grandpa's squeaky wheel returned.

This comedy routine repeated itself several times until my frustrated dad sniped, "Would you be still!?"

Grandpa froze and took his mild scolding, as my still agitated father yanked his second shot into a mammoth pine tree. The ball made a sharp cracking sound as it ricocheted off the tree and into the sand bunker. Dad, who prided himself on always being in control of his anger compared to my frequent outbursts, slammed his iron back into the bag, while muttering some unintelligible comment under his breath as he stormed up the hill to play his third shot.

I stood there as a rare witness to someone else losing their temper.

Grandpa, with a mischievous smirk, turned to me and said, "I see where you get your temper, now."

I managed to muffle my laughter and walked up the fairway with Grandpa, realizing maybe golf was best played as a game, after all. Like life, golf is rarely fair, but you learn to take what the course gives you that day. It was years before I could enjoy the game as my grandfather had. Some would argue I never really conquered my fierce temper: I only learned to disguise it. As I am older now, I have a greater appreciation for those precious hours spent with the two men that helped make me into the person I eventually became. Grandpa had been right. I probably did inherit some of my father's competitiveness. I like to think I also received some of his determination and perspective on life. It's said that with age comes wisdom, but on the golf course, sometimes age comes alone.

THE END

THE PREACHER

"What would you know about that, Preacher?" Jeremy Finley asks, in an almost angry tone.

Jeremy, a young man not yet twenty, stares at the preacher while he holds on to a broken-down mule with a shabby saddle on its back. The man they called Preacher, was born Jack Cutter, but had been called several names during his life. Preacher showed up several years ago to minister to his small congregation in this backwoods town tucked miles away from anything resembling a city. He wore a neatly trimmed, graying beard and had a round face that resembled General Robert E. Lee to some extent. He was a simple man, and Jeremy had never seen him in anything but his modest brown suit. He'd been a good preacher. The people in town respected him, even if few of them attended his small congregation made of poor folks trying to survive the times.

"I know what's right and what's wrong," Preacher replied. "So, do you."

Jeremy huffs, "It weren't but three dollars and fifty cents. Old man Moody wastes that much playing poker Friday nights. I thought he'd never miss it."

Preacher sighs heavily before saying, "A man like Tom Moody doesn't find success like he has without knowing how to count his money. He's threatened to turn you over to the sheriff in Tecumseh unless you pay him back." Preacher looks over the old mule before continuing, "Looks like you have a notion to skip town. Do you think that's a good idea?"

The younger man looks at his feet a moment before saying, "Don't know if'n it's a good idea or not, but it seems I'm out of options. Times are hard, Preacher. You know that. This town ain't got nothing for me. I need a fresh start."

Preacher studies him carefully and then asks, "You think running away will do that? You really think you have nothing here at all? How about Mary Jane? Have you thought of what this will do to her?"

Jeremy slouches slightly in his shoulders before answering, "I don't know, Preacher. I just don't know anymore."

Preacher smiles mischievously as he says, "I do know, and running away won't solve any of your problems. You're a good boy, Jeremy. I remember the day you were baptized. You couldn't have been more than twelve. It was one of my first weeks at the church. I saw goodness in you that day. I think the Lord still sees it in you."

Jeremy had been the first soul Preacher had saved. He had been nervous that first sermon, but the boy responded. Preacher liked the boy immediately and had kept an eye on him. The boy's father died in an accident not long after he was born. The family struggled, and Preacher knew the stress had been hard on the boy.

"You don't know as much as you think," Jeremy huffs.

"I might surprise you," Preacher smiles. "This depression's been tough on a lot of folks around here. It causes people to rationalize some pretty disturbing behavior. They say table manners get awful bad when there's not enough beans to go around. For a young fella, the easy way always seems the best way. You see Tom Moody havin' a little more than anyone else and think he won't miss a few dollars. But it's more than the money. It's about the choices you make. You're a man now, and the choices you make will determine your future. You don't want to go down the path you're taking. It don't lead anywhere you want to be."

"It ain't that easy," Jeremy moans. "You don't know the half of it."

"The Good Book teaches, 'Confession is good for the soul,'" Preacher suggests. "Why don't you try telling me about it?"

Jeremy frowns and slides his worn boot in the dirt before saying, "Today weren't the first time."

"You mean today's the first time you got caught?"

"Yeah."

Preacher studies the boy before saying, "The first step to repentance is realizing we need a change. Maybe it's a good thing you got caught today. How much have you stole?"

Jeremy hesitates before answering, "I took seventy-five cents about two weeks ago. No one seemed to notice much so, I've been taking a dollar here and there."

"How much?" Preacher demands.

"I don't know," Jeremy groans. "Maybe twelve—fifteen dollars in all."

Preacher rubs his chin before asking, "We'll get to the girl later, but are you telling me the truth, son? Would fifteen dollars get you square with Tom Moody?"

Jeremy nods.

"How much do you have of it?" Preacher inquires.

"Almost two dollars," Jeremy confesses.

"You spent the rest of it?" Preacher asks.

Jeremy nods.

"What on?"

Jeremy shrugs, "Stuff. Some tobacco—a little food."

"Gambling?"

"A little," Jeremy admits. "I went to the domino parlor with the old men, but didn't have much luck."

"I don't suspect you did with that bunch," Preacher smirks.

Jeremy nods sheepishly, somewhat embarrassed about how much the preacher knows about his vices.

Preacher lets him stew for a while then says slowly, "You didn't get much for your thievery, did you?"

Jeremy shakes his head as he stares at the bare ground below his feet. "Not as much as I need. My problem calls for a lot more than fifteen dollars. I know that now. The bank's about to foreclose on the farm. Mom—she's got family back in Arkansas, but they don't have no need for me. It'd take five hundred dollars to put the farm back to profitable."

"You plan to skedaddle out of town on this broken down old mule," Preacher suggests. "You think your luck might be better somewhere else. You got caught, so you decided to run."

"When Mom leaves, I don't have no family that counts for much," Jeremy defends. "I've heard about prison in McAlester. I can't make it there. I didn't know what else to do."

"You could've come to me," Preacher scolds. "You could've done a little confessing before you got caught by Tom Moody. That'd been a better plan."

"No offense, Preacher," Jeremy defends, "but I didn't figure you'd be much help with the problems I got."

Preacher straightens up and controls a wicked grin as he says, "I haven't always been an old man. I was young once—I remember. That's the problem with you young folks. You forget us old timers have been your age and know a little about mischief. You, on the other hand, know nothing about growing old. The question is, what do we do now?"

Jeremy shakes his head and says, "I don't want prison, and I see no mercy coming from Mr. Moody. I think I better take my two dollars and this old mule and try somewheres else."

"And Mary Ann?"

"What about Mary Ann?" Jeremy fumes. "What does she got to do with this? She'd be better off if I'm gone. Her family would agree with that."

"You've said sweet things to that girl?" Preacher surmises.

"How'd you know about that?" Jeremy angrily protests.

"I'm the preacher. People tell me things. Besides—I got eyes. I've seen you two together. I know how love works on young people."

"How could you know?" Jeremy objects. "I ain't ever seen you with no woman."

Preacher doesn't respond for a long moment, but finally confides, "I had a good woman, one time. The kind of woman that no other woman could ever replace. She passed on, but her memory is always with me. She's still the better part of me, when I listen. And it's a good thing for you, because the man in me wants to give you a thrashing right here and now, but her gentleness is telling me to be patient with you. So, I'll listen—even though it's hard sometimes."

"I didn't know," Jeremy groans.

"Well, that's the thing about bein' a preacher. People tell you a great deal about their troubles, but don't get around much to knowing about yours. That's one of the things I like about spreadin' the gospel, I guess."

"I'm sorry. I truly am," Jeremy says.

"I believe you are and accept your apology," Preacher smiles. "Now back to Mary Ann. There's worse things than a broken heart a man can leave a woman with. You and that girl have been pretty familiar. Anything else you running from?"

Jeremy grimaces, "I may have said some things. I may have made some promises."

Preacher studies the young man before stepping away to think about the situation. He had helped others struggling with their spiritual wellbeing, but this boy's closer to him. The preacher wondered to himself why life seemed so hard for some. He needed to deliver an impactful sermon to the boy, but struggled with how he could do that. What bothered him the most were the things his congregation would never know about his past.

"We find ourselves in quite a pickle," Preacher begins. "You've got to take responsibility for your choices—there's no getting around that. People repent when they realize they have to make a change. They have to change their behavior and then the hard part—they have to be resilient to continue on the good path. Repentance is not easy—it's plumb hard sometimes, but it's the only way. I guess my question to you is: are you sorry for stealing and putting that girl in the way you have, or are you just sorry you got caught? With one answer, I can help you out. With the other, all I can do is give you a prediction about where your life will be— here and in eternity."

Jeremy looks nervously at the preacher and says, "I don't know. I feel sorry for a whole lot, and everything seems to be pushing down on me."

Preacher nods, "That's at least an honest answer. Truth is, you probably don't know. But let me tell you what your future will be if you're just sorry for being caught and think you're a smart guy that can fool the old preacher. If you keep on with these theivin' ways you're going to hook up with people that don't think any more about others than you do. You'll find a life where stealin, and lyin', and killin', and all kinds of debauchery will seem normal. You'll never feel right, but you'll always be looking for something that's not there. In the end, you'll be hunted like an animal, locked up like an animal, and start to believe you're nothing but an animal. You'll find friends like the prodigal did that will be there when the good times seem to be happening, but they'll vanish like the dew in the morning, and someday, you'll want to go home and there'll be no way back. There's still a way back for you now, but you have to make some hard choices—today. I guess I do too."

"What do I do, Preacher?" Jeremy laments. "I can't see clear to know for myself."

"Can you change your ways?" Preacher pointedly asks.

"I can try," Jeremy replies.

Preacher watches him closely for a few seconds before saying, "You get on your knees tonight and ask God to forgive you. You tell Him you've learned He's in charge and that you've made a mess of things on your own. I'll go talk to Tom Moody this afternoon and see if I can make things straight with him. It won't be a pleasant conversation, but I can talk his language. I doubt you'll get your job back with him or any other merchant, but I have some favors owed me at the grist mill, and I think I can get you some work there—if you're willing to work hard."

Jeremy nods.

"You meet me tomorrow morning at the Federal National Bank in Tecumseh," Preacher commands. "I got a little money saved, and I'm going to give you a loan that you can pay back when you can. I expect you to make things right with that girl. The money'll give you enough to pay back Tom Moody and a little stake to help you start over."

"Why are doing this for me?" Jeremy asks.

Preacher smiles, "You said you didn't have much luck gambling at the domino parlor. I never had much luck either with cards or dice. I decided a long time ago to bet on people. I'm wagering I know you better than you know yourself. I'm betting on you Jeremy. I figure it's time someone did."

"Thanks," Jeremy nods.

"You meet me at the bank at ten o'clock sharp," Preacher commands. "We'll straighten things out."

Jeremy nods and walks away.

Preacher met that afternoon with Tom Moody. It took some persuasion, but he convinced the businessman to take his repayment and keep the sheriff out of the matter. He spent his evening straightening up the simple room he kept in the back of the small church building. He wrote a few letters and wondered what the morning would bring. He hoped the boy would meet him at the bank, but knew there was an equally good chance he would try to run from his problems.

The morning was clear and bright as he waited outside the bank in Tecumseh. He had shaved for the first time in years and put on a suit of clothes he had not worn in a long time. The pants were too tight, but the suit coat covered up his bulges. He paced nervously as ten o'clock came and went. The boy was a no show, but Preacher couldn't give up that easily. It was ten minutes before he saw Jeremy Finley walk slowly toward the entrance to the bank.

"Jeremy," Preacher greets, as the boy walked by him.

The confused boy stops and stares at the man who had been his preacher for nearly eight years. "Preacher?" he finally asks, as he realizes the man greeting him is not a stranger. "I didn't recognize you dressed like that and–I've never seen you shaved before. You look different."

"I thought I needed a change today," Preacher smiles. "I bought this suit in Kansas City and thought it needed to be worn today. I—I about decided you'd chosen to run away from your problems. I'm glad to see you this morning."

"I thought about it," Jeremy admits. "I did what you said and got on my knees and prayed. I had a million thoughts goin' through my head, but decided you were right—I got to make things right with Mary Ann—I got to make things right with myself."

Preacher nods as he grins, "I hoped you'd make that choice. Let's go into the bank and do our business."

Jeremy nods and follows Preacher into the bank. Preacher looks different than Jeremy had ever seen. He's clean shaven, and his hair is slick with Brylcreem®. Preacher looks younger, and even his gait is different this day. He walks with a confidence that almost seems like a swagger. Preacher's suit doesn't fit so well, but it looks more as if he's on his way to a Saturday night party than a Sunday morning sermon.

Walking up to the first teller, Preacher says, "I need to see Mr. Williams. He owns the bank, doesn't he?"

"Yes, sir," the teller replies, "but he's a busy man. Who can I say is here to see him?"

Preacher looks at Jeremy before announcing, "Tell him Jeremy Finley is here to square the mortgage on his family's farm."

The teller sends a message back, and the two men wait patiently for nearly ten minutes before a clerk steps outside the cage to invite them back. Mr. Williams keeps a small, but nicely furnished, office close to the bank's vault.

"What can I do for you?" Mr. Williams tersely asks, as he motions for the two visitors to sit.

Preacher says calmly, "You hold the mortgage on the Finley place south of Macomb?"

"I do," Mr. Williams confirms. "It's past due, and I've got papers to file to repossess."

"I suspect, as a banker, you would prefer payment," Preacher suggests. "In full?"

"Of course," Mr. Williams replies. "The last thing I need is another farm to liquidate, but—the bank has not had any payment since the first of this year."

"Could you tell me the balance," Preacher asks, "with interest?"

Mr. Williams leaves his desk for a moment before returning with a handful of papers. After carefully surveying them, he says, "The balance due is nearly $140 dollars to stop foreclosure."

"What's the total due to clear the mortgage?" Preacher asks.

Mr. Williams hesitates, as if he will ask a question, before searching his papers again to say, "The entire mortgage is $617.87 to pay in full—today."

"We don't owe more than $500!" Jeremy interjects.

Mr. Williams quickly responds in a practiced way, "You owed that two years ago, but interest mounts up and $617.87 is the amount owed. I have an obligation to the shareholders and depositors of the bank to protect their assets."

"And your own," Preacher smirks.

"Mine and the banks," Mr. Williams declares.

"I think Mr. Finley here will have the banks money by the end of the week, if that's okay with you?" Preacher states.

Mr. Williams looks at the poorly clothed boy with a dubious glare as he says, "If that's possible, I'd be glad to release the mortgage."

"It's done then," Preacher declares.

"It's too much," Jeremy whispers. "I'd never be able to pay you back."

"Let me worry about that," Preacher smiles.

"I admire your intentions," Mr. Williams interrupts, "but do you have that kind of cash on hand? I'm well aware of all accounts in my bank and pretty familiar with any large deposits in all the banks of the county."

Preacher stares sternly at Mr. Williams in an almost threatening manner. "Call up the Pinkertons. Find Byron Lattimore, if you must. I hear he's still in the state. Tell 'em Jeremy Finley has brought in Jack Cutter."

When Preacher announces his name, a shift in attitude immediately strikes the banker. It is as if he has seen a ghost. Jeremy has never experienced sheer terror, but he sees it in the banker's face.

Preacher, who had revealed himself as Jack Cutter, calmly states, "There should be a reward of at least $1,000 from the banking association. The money belongs to the boy."

"Preacher—" Jeremy starts to plead, before Jack Cutter interrupts him.

Jack Cutter states to Mr. Williams, "You might want to tell the sheriff or someone in authority that I'll be at the City Café. I won't cause no trouble and will come peaceable."

Mr. Williams now stares at Jack Cutter before saying, "Is it really you?"

"You can bet it is," Preacher smirks. "And if I was fifteen years younger, I'd be leaving your bank with all your deposits. This is your lucky day."

Without further discussion Preacher rises from his chair, which causes Mr. Williams to recoil. He takes Jeremy by the arm and quickly drags the boy out of the bank, across the street, and to a table in the back of the City Café.

"I don't understand," Jeremy moans, as he takes his seat with his back to the front door.

"We'll have two coffees," Preacher orders, as the tired waitress approaches. "I'll have an egg sandwich with that. You want anything, Jeremy?"

Jeremy shakes his head.

"Two coffees and the egg sandwich, then," Preacher says to the waitress. "And you better make that quickly."

"What are you doing?" Jeremy asks.

Preacher thinks for second before replying, "Paying a debt I owe. A debt to you."

"Why?"

Preacher touches the side of his head where his hair had been cut close to his temple as he says, "Life's about consequences and rewards—it's about the choices we make. I made mine a long time ago. I've tried to make amends, and think I did pretty well, but it's time for me to pay in full, now."

"Who's Jack Cutter?" Jeremy asks.

"It's still strange hearing that name," Preacher sighs. "Jack the Cutter, they used to call me, because I could cut a man in two with a Tommy gun. I was a bank robber of some repute before I mended my ways. I think our friend Mr. Williams believed I still was a robber."

"That can't be," Jeremy protests. "I've known you most of my life. You're the preacher."

"I was with your father when he died," Preacher solemnly confesses.

"At his accident?" Jeremy asks.

Preacher nods, "Only it weren't an accident. Your father had made the same bad choices I had. He'd run with the same bad people I did. I don't think we ever started out to be bad people, but the path we took made it inevitable. We took up with James Overstreet. Some called him the Jellybean bandit, and some the Swell Kid, but he was never no kid. We robbed the bank in Shawnee in '24. Would've gotten away with it too, if Overstreet could have kept his temper under control. We were at a cemetery near Bristow dead near midnight. It was cold, and we were fussing about dividing up the money. Your daddy fussed a little too much, and James shot him in the back of the head. He asked, 'Any more questions?' We were all too numb to answer. We knew the money was his, and it would just be a matter of time before he shot us in the back, as well.

"You see—men like James Overstreet can seem to be your best friend, but you got to realize they're always in it for themselves. They have no conscience, unless they're caught, or trapped, or it's to their advantage. Overstreet took a shot at me, but only nicked my leg. I managed to escape. He was caught a few days later in Fort Worth. I made it to a farm after nearly bleeding to death. That's where I met my Helen. She was a good woman—a preacher's daughter that never asked too many questions, but accepted me as I was. I found myself with her and decided to try a new life. She's the one that taught me the Bible. We were going to have a baby, but Helen didn't make it when the time came. I lost her and my daughter. I was angry at the world, and God, and everyone, but knew deep inside it was all on me.

"After a few weeks of mourning and praying, I decided to do what my Helen would have wanted me to do. I took some of her father's preaching books he had left her and made my way to Macomb. I found a rundown old building with a few women needing a preacher—your mother was one of those women. I figured I owed her something—figured I owed you something too, since I couldn't save your father. When you responded to my first poor sermon I gave on that first Sunday, I knew I had found my calling."

"You can't do this," Jeremy protests. "You can still get away. It's been a long time since you've been a robber. They won't chase you for long. You can start over someplace new."

Preacher sighs, "Can't do it. I see the path you've started, and it's the same one your father and I took. It leads to no future. You were right. Prison is no place for you. It would break a kid like you and only make you harder and meaner."

"Don't you see?" Jeremy declares. "That's where they'll send you!"

Preacher nods, "I've been there before. I'm an old man. Prison can't hurt me much. The Good Lord said he came to minister to the sick, not the well. I figure maybe my preaching skills might be needed as much in McAlester as anywhere. You're a good boy. I've seen it. Confession is good for the soul. I feel better having told you some of the things about my past that brought me to where I am. I've done a lot of bad things in my life. More than I've told you about. More than my Helen ever could have imagined. I got a second chance because of her. I'm giving that gift to you now. I'll only ask one thing."

"What's that?" Jeremy asks.

"Try as best you can to live for the good of others more than yourself," Preacher implores. "We all make a choice to be the selfish people we tend to be or the selfless person we can be. Mary Ann can show you how to be the person you can be."

Preacher stops and puts up his hands before continuing, "I didn't get that last sandwich. The sheriff's here. Take the reward money—the Pinkertons will pay it—and live your life. That's all I can do for you."

Without much commotion, the Pottawatomie County Sheriff escorted Jack Cutter—Preacher—out the door of the City Café and to the county jail. Jeremy sat silently at the table, and after a while, the café returned to its normal lunch business.

"You want this egg sandwich your friend ordered?" the waitress asks.

Jeremy thinks for a second before frowning, "Could you wrap it up? I've got business at the courthouse."

THE END

THE BULLY

The old school had been safe. My friends all came from the same neighborhood—our parents were all friends. Kindergarten to sixth grade felt right. It seemed like I belonged.

Central Junior High was the opposite. It was big—a three story building looking more like a prison than a school. Strangers lurked everywhere with unfamiliar teachers and students. The halls were crowded, and the institution had a cold, hard feeling. Many of us seventh-graders were still boys, while some of the ninth-graders looked like men. Junior high girls came in all shapes and sizes, but all seemed more mature and completely out of reach for those of us in seventh-grade. Even my friends that were girls from the old school changed over the summer. The pretty ones were showered with attention from the older boys. I had never felt more alone.

Some of my old friends were into sports, others the band. It appeared one of the main purposes of junior high was to divide us into groups. I belonged nowhere. As my old friends made new friends, I tried to survive with all the different factions. I believed in my first few days it was my only strategy.

My painful initiation to the realities of junior high happened in the lunchroom on the second day. It was a one-two punch: the first from a friend and the second from an enemy. While standing in line to buy milk to go with the lunch I carried from home, Mark Sherman saw me in line and turned the other way. I had known Mark since first grade. He played football and quickly joined that group. We had not been best friends, but we had played Hot Wheels® the summer before last. I didn't want anything from Mark but a wave hello or an acknowledgement I existed. He couldn't risk being seen with a non-athlete like me. He did the worst thing he could have done that day—he ignored me.

As I pouted in line, the second blow hit me. Though offended when Mark ignored me, I wanted to be left alone when Lyle Dutton approached. Lyle was a surly boy that stood half-a-head taller than most in the school. I was at least a half-a-head shorter. He had muscles, whiskers on his upper lip, and a small scar above his right eye. Everything about him looked tough, and hard, and mean. I heard stories about him and knew to keep my distance. As I consciously turned to avoid eye contact, I saw him walking toward me. I did not dare look him in the eye, but had the uneasy feeling he was coming for me.

"Hey!" he huffed, in a deep, but subdued voice.

I turned to check my surroundings to see who might be this bully's unfortunate victim. A quick survey did not look promising. I failed to see one kid responding, or even in my immediate area.

"Hey!" he repeated, with more urgency.

As I continued to ignore the greeting that I hoped was intended for someone else, I turned the wrong way to come face to chest with him. I slowly looked up to see Lyle's dark eyes glaring at me. His eyes looked like that of a shark, as the deadly fish might stalk its unfortunate prey. His mouth seemed to snarl, and he stood much closer to me than was comfortable.

"I'm talking to you," he announced forcefully. After one last attempt to see if there was possibly anyone else he was there to intimidate, he continued, "Are you deaf or something?"

"No," I managed to mumble.

Lyle glared at me a moment that seemed to last an hour before saying, "I need a quarter for milk."

It had not been the first time I had been asked for money at Central Junior High. I had developed a reflex to deny I had any extra change, but never to anyone as big as Lyle.

"I don't have any," I muttered.

"I just saw the lunch lady give you change," Lyle redirected.

"Oh," I sighed.

"Come on man," Lyle coaxed. "Can you give me a quarter?" After a hesitation, he added, "I'll pay you back."

A quarter seemed a small price to pay for my life so I dug into my pocket for the change. I pulled out two quarters and was surprised when Lyle took only one.

"Thanks," he murmured. "I'll catch you tomorrow."

With that, Lyle Dutton let me live for the day. I scanned the room to see if anyone else had seen my near-death experience. Everyone clamored in the chaos of the lunchroom, indifferent to my encounter. I did see one small kid look at me and shake his head as if relieved he had skipped the intimidation for the day.

The rest of the week did not go better at the new school. Everyone had found their group, and I felt even more isolated. I did run into my old friend Mark a couple of times. He would nod—at least when no one else was around. He was embarrassed to be seen with me, but at least he acknowledged me sometimes. My memory of junior high classwork is vague to me now, but I learned how to navigate to my locker, find class, and most importantly, dodge bullies like Lyle Dutton.

Lyle had seen me from a distance a couple of times, but I managed to retreat quickly and avoid more pleas for money or threats of getting beat up. By the second week, I had learned Lyle's schedule and carefully managed my routes around school to avoid any place he might be, including the lunchroom. I found a secluded spot outside to cower as I ate the lunch I brought. Eating my sandwich without milk was safer than risking an encounter with Lyle. I was not alone. Everyone in school feared him—even the smoker hiding out by the trash dumpsters. I was surviving, but every day presented challenges.

Thursday started off badly. First, Mrs. Anderson kept me after class third hour to discuss my failures in the daily assignment. I didn't mind her correction, but she sabotaged my schedule. After third hour, I would race to my secluded corner to gobble lunch and avoid Lyle, who inconveniently had my lunch period.

I took a back way to my secluded sanctuary. The cackle of adolescent football players should have been a warning, but I thought I could pass the group without being noticed.

"What are you looking at?" a tall boy demanded, as he quickly rolled up a magazine the gang had congregated to see.

"Nothing," I stammer.

"You look like a nark," another chided.

Two of them move closer to block my way.

"I'm just going to lunch," I sighed.

"You were spying on us," the tall boy sneered.

"No," I defended.

"Leave him alone," the familiar voice of Mark Sherman timidly requested.

"Is this brainiac a friend of yours?" my tormenter challenged.

Mark looked at me briefly before saying, "Naw, man. But, he's harmless."

"If he's harmless then, let's take him to the pole!" one of the group shouted.

Without warning, two of the players grabbed my arms. My lunch and books dropped to the ground as I thrashed to free myself. Mark took a step back, as his new friends dragged me to somewhere I didn't want to go.

"Stop it!" I pleaded pathetically, which only excited the gang.

"Or what?" the one of them teased. "You going to tell on us? I wouldn't do that, if I were you."

"Let him go!" a strange voice from several steps away demanded.

I slunk to the ground in humiliation, thankful that some teacher or principal was finally coming to my rescue. The two beasts holding me firmly under the armpits hesitated a second before tossing me to the ground. I scrambled to find my glasses, but when I did, I could see Lyle Dutton walking forcefully toward me. The group of boys stood motionless, as they held their ground.

"What do you want?" the tall boy asked Lyle.

Lyle did not answer, but continued to approach, eventually nudging the players out of the way to stand over me. He wasn't there to rescue me, but to lay claim to my beating since I had successfully avoided him for a week.

"Heard you might play football," the tall boy announced. "Coach said we could use someone like you on the D line."

Lyle continued his silence as he reached down to pick me off the ground.

"Hey, man, I'm talking to you," the tall boy stated, with a slight tone of agitation.

Lyle looked at me and asked, "You okay?"

I managed to nod, as he continued to hold me firmly by the upper arm.

One of the players stepped in front of Lyle to sneer, "You disrespecting us?"

Lyle showed no emotion as he forcefully shoved the boy, causing him to stumble to the ground.

"If you want to take it that way," Lyle stoically stated.

The boy hopped up to face Lyle, but did not approach. "Let's get out of here," he said to his small gang.

Mark was the last to move, but he went along with the group.

"Let me make myself clear," Lyle announced. "You mess with this kid, you mess with me."

"Whatever," the blond boy replied, but without breaking stride in his retreat.

Lyle let go of my arm as he said, "You sure you're alright?"

I nod.

"You've been avoiding me," Lyle said.

I shake my head to deny his observation, although he spoke the truth.

Lyle did not challenge me, but instead said, "I owe you a quarter. I've been trying to catch you all week. What did you do to those guys?"

"Nothing," I said. "I was walking around the building and ran into them."

"Brave guys in a group," Lyle said.

"You weren't afraid of them," I replied.

Lyle almost smiled, "I'm bigger than most of them. I guess I look kind of tough, because no one's bothered me much."

"They wouldn't," I confirmed.

"You eating lunch?" Lyle asked. "I owe you a milk."

I nod my acceptance. Lyle Dutton and I had lunch together for the first time that day. We would have many lunches for the rest of our school days. Despite coming from separate parts of town, having diverse personalities, and obviously different physiques, we discovered we had more in common than different. We both liked science fiction, going to the movies, and making comments about the peculiarities of other people's behavior. Lyle went on to play football, but never let it be barrier to who he was. Mark Sherman apologized to me later in the year, but we were never more than acquaintances in high school.

The day Lyle Dutton stood up for me was the day I discovered much about myself. I couldn't be afraid anymore. I wouldn't let others dictate how I felt about myself. I learned from Lyle Dutton, that what people do is much more important than what they say. I tried to never let my first impressions of a person influence my opinion of someone before I took the time to know and understand them. The day Lyle paid me back for milk money turned out to be the day I found my best friend.

THE END

THE OLD PEAR TREE

"Cut it down, Ernest!" Mom pleaded to Dad.

Dad shook his head and smiled mockingly, "Naw. She's lasted this long. We'll keep her a few more years."

My parents stood in front of a gnarled and weathered pear tree toward the back of our large fenced yard on the 160 acres Dad bought that summer. He had saved for years to make a down payment on the farm and intended to make a go of it here. Mom was supportive, but wanted to make improvements to the house and yard: particularly the removal of an old pear tree close to the rusting barbwire fence, which separated the yard from the fields. Our yard included a small garden, two apple trees, two peach trees, one good pear tree, and the twisted wreck of a tree Mom wanted removed.

Mom was right. Even as a boy of eleven, I thought the tree ugly and useless. The scarred trunk was about a foot in diameter and looked as if several attempts had already been made to destroy it. The crooked limbs knotted together in an impossible labyrinth, which made it useless for my brothers and me to climb. The contorted branches grew straight toward the sky before bending awkwardly toward the ground. Dead limbs increased the ugliness of the tree. The bent and knotted branches made it difficult to prune in any orderly fashion. My older brother and Dad could have cut the tree down in an hour to make Mom happy, but Dad was uncharacteristically stubborn and refused.

"That tree is a disgrace," Mom complained. "It makes the rest of the property look—poor. Won't you please cut it down?"

Dad stood under the shade of the tree and examined it like a veterinarian might look at a horse before saying, "My knees are kind of knobby and bowed. Do you want to cut me down too?"

"I might, if you don't get rid of that tree," Mom fumed.

Dad laughed, "It might come to that. This place needs a lot of work, and taking this tree out is not high on my priority list right now. As the seasons changed, Mom's pleas to remove the tree intensified to the point of her threatening to take the axe to it herself. Dad would smile and encourage her to do so, but maintain that he liked the tree. It became their daily battle.

"Why do you do it?" I asked, one day. "Why do you tease Mom about this old tree?"

Dad pondered my question as if deciding how much he should tell a boy, who was not yet a man, about his marital relationship. "Your maw and me are two peas in a pod," Dad explained. "We understand each other in a way that generally doesn't need to be spoken. We get along so well, and agree on so much, I find it healthy to have something as senseless as this old tree to argue about."

I looked at the disfigured tree as I said, "I guess so, but I'll have to agree with Mom that it sure is an ugly tree."

Dad laughed, "We'll see. Don't be too hasty to judge things— or people by their appearance."

In my thirteenth year, the dust bowl nearly consumed us. It was hot, dusty, and dire. Dad managed to harvest a small crop, but it was hardly worth the effort. Mom kept the garden watered enough to feed us. The fruit trees were all nearly bare, except for that wicked pear tree Mom had all but cursed for the previous years.

Seems the gnarled pear tree grew close enough to the lateral lines to get some hidden nourishment. The pears were so thick the branches and limbs bent low to the ground, emphasizing the twist personality of the tree. Mom harvested the pears in late summer to make pear preserves while still muttering about the grotesque aesthetics of the tree. As my blushing mother accepted the blue ribbon at the county fair that fall for her preserves, my dad smirked at being right about the old pear tree.

"How did you know?" I asked, while Mom basked in her accolades.

Dad answered, "I didn't know, but I suspected. That old pear tree's limbs bent toward the ground telling me it had born a lot of fruit at some time. I figured it had a chance to have a bumper crop again, if conditions were right. I guess this drought forced enough raccoons away that this was the year it produced. Look at your mom. She's proud as a soldier about her ribbon, but dreading my teasing about being right about the tree."

"Will you?" I asked. "I mean—will you tease her on the way home about the tree."

"Naw," Dad declared. "Sometimes the anticipation of something is better or worse than the event. I'll let your mom enjoy her award. She'll worry about what I might say, because it's her nature to worry—but I won't say anything. You'll be married some day and understand."

I nodded, although not fully appreciating the wisdom of my dad then. The old wicked pear tree my mom hated and learned to love, died before I left home. Without any emotion, Dad cut it down to the roots and burned the remains. Mom cried that day.

I grew up and left the farm, got an education, and started a family of my own. I found my place in the city and succeeded in business. I came back to the farm as often as I could to visit the folks. My dad had bowed legs and slouching shoulders from his years of hard labor on the farm by then. I was considered successful in business, but always deferred any real questions of importance to Dad. Like the old pear tree, he had stood the test of time and always seemed to have one more gift of advice for me— one more thing I could learn from his life lived well.

THE END

The Diary of Nurse Amber

And...it begins!!! I can't believe they talked me into being camp nurse again. The whining and the crying and the temper tantrums are hard to take—and that's from the counselors. Campers are nearly as immature.

Day 1 at Burnt Cabin Youth Camp!

We start with torrential rain, add 90 degrees, and it equals perfect weather—for a sauna! Unloading supplies, checking kids for lice, asking about medications, reading cryptic maternal instructions, and...learning about allergies.

One kid writes, "My allergies make my eyes itchy but they don't make me die."

Not really sure how to manage the kiddo whose camp application states they are allergic to: "Outside Air."

Another first-year junior camper wearing long pants in this steam bath says, "I think I'm allergic to peanuts."

Me, "You think?"

The camper timidly nods, "I don't like peanut butter, so I must be allergic."

What kind of kid doesn't like peanut butter? I think to myself. What I say with an exaggerated sigh, "That's not an allergy, but thanks for sharing, kid."

The boy then hands me a note from his mother with detailed instructions for his care—no peanut allergy listed.

A junior camper, "Nurse Amber, I have a headache."

Me, "You homesick already?"

Junior camper nods, "Uh-huh."

Me, "We have been here LESS THAN 3 HOURS! Go, drink some water, and find a friend!"

Camper hands me his medications.

Me, "What do you take this for?"

Junior boy, "I'm not sure but if I don't take it I could die!"

I guess that one's important.

The power of Zyrtec, Miralax, and every ADHD medication the FDA has ever approved is essential to my sanity. I've already witnessed a couple of campers who need a higher dosage than prescribed.

While checking kids in for the week, I discover three "camper babies" this year. You see, parents can send their offspring to camp when they are nine years old. A "camper baby" has a March birthday and an older brother or sister in the senior cabin who is eighteen. Do the math. Mom and dad shipped the older kid to camp for a little rest and relaxation, and presto! They have another kid to send to camp nine years later.

Several lifesaving Band-Aids have already been applied, one loose tooth removed, two headaches diagnosed (one was a headache a camper had, and the other will be a headache for the counselors), more bug bites than I care to keep track of, and two cases of extreme home-sick-I-need-my-mommy syndrome!

Now to create organization out of chaos! I have two hours of work before lights out. Then another two hours after that dealing with any faux-illness and hypochondriac condition known to mankind. It's going to be a long week!

NURSE AMBER-OUT!

<u>Day 2 at Burnt Cabin Youth Camp. (The exclamation point from Day 1 is purposefully left off.)</u>

What did I do to deserve this? Bug bites are dominating these kids. Two more teeth lost and given to me—several bouts of swimmers' ear.

Camper tells me, "I need you to know that I have an eating disorder, I really can't eat if I'm hot or sweaty." Me thinks this kid may not survive the week!

Down at the ball field. Camper complains in all seriousness, "I don't think my mom would want me to be this sweaty."

Junior boy tells me, "I don't know why we don't just play this on the Wii. I'm really good at that!"

Intermediate camper, "Nurse Amber? Did you have to go to college to learn how to put Band-Aids on good?"

The power of Band-Aids. I used to think they were just a bandage to cover a wound and help keep it clean. At camp, Band-Aids are essential and life-sustaining. They have a healing power for all kinds of physical, emotional, and psychological ailments. I'm thinking of putting one on my head.

If anyone knows how to take out a splinter without touching the splinter or the toe that it is in, please let me know. It's a skill they didn't teach me in nursing school nor one that I've acquired in 20 years of experience!

Speaking of experience, today was a first. The "I think I have a peanut butter allergy kid," with extensive instructions from his mom comes hopping up (literally) to say, "My foot came off." I have learned to be skeptical and sigh heavily until I notice the kid is holding a foot in his hand! I go into full panic mode, but the little camper is taking it all in stride—while literally holding his foot in his hand! (I know I repeated myself, but the camper is HOLDING—HIS—FOOT—IN—HIS—HAND!)

Come to find out, the kid had an accident when he was younger and has a prosthetic lower leg. Mom forgot to mention this in her extensive instructions, and the kid has learned to deal with it. I should have known something was up when he was wearing blue jeans in the middle of summer. Joe the handyman has a wrench. We bolt the foot back on. Nothing to see here!

Counselors are a problem all to themselves. We've got one guy who must dream of being a drill sergeant. He yells at kids constantly. I just call him "Yelling Guy," since what I'd really like to name him seems inappropriate at church camp. He's somewhat out of shape and comes to see me complaining of muscle soreness and joint pain—also known as old age. I sneak him an 800 mg ibuprofen. He gobbles it up and looks guilty like he's getting his opium fix from a drug dealer. He'll be looking me up every day for the rest of the week. The other extreme is "Kumbaya Girl" who appears to be a misplaced hippie from the '60s that is filled with so much love and peace and happiness that it makes me ill. She's barely twenty, but seems to have all the answers to life's important questions already. Oh well. People and counselors come in all kinds.

Most of the work of a camp nurse is explaining to campers and counselors that things are going to be all right, and your condition is not really a big deal—until today. Besides the camper holding his foot in his hand, another boy complains of belly pain. It really is a problem. We make a mad dash to the ER, a helicopter ride to Tulsa, emergency surgery for something serious, and (deep sigh) now all is well.

Until…I come back to my cabin to a note written on a paper towel on the toilet seat in my bathroom saying, "I violated your toilet. I didn't have time to fix it. You wouldn't want me to be late to Bible class."

If they had signed it, I would have killed them…and then treated them. Hand me a plunger and show me the shower. I've had enough for the day!

NURSE AMBER-OUT! (With a strong exclamation point!!!)

Day 3 of Burnt Cabin Youth Camp (too tired for any punctuation)

Woke up with little pieces of circa 1960 popcorn ceiling falling on my face/hair—and barely noticed. I'm so tired.

Started off with a little ingrown toenail surgery this morning, complete with pus and white knuckles, and of course a crowd of the camper's homies making obnoxious observations! One passed out, though. That causes me to smirk.

Yelling Guy is starting to get on my nerves. I may need to give him a healthy dose of something to chill him out along with his ibuprofen fix. I'm thinking Benadryl might do the trick. That would be better for him than a softball bat to the head. Never fear, Kumbaya Girl is playing the guitar and singing to the kids. Oh, if only I had a medication for her.

Overheard a conversation that went like this:

"Why didn't Cloe come back this year?"

"I don't know."

"Didn't she have a good time?"

"She had the time of her life."

Another camper interrupts (a camp tradition), "Her mom said she came back home last year with too many tick bites."

I've lost count of how many ticks I've pulled off these kids and how many bug bites I've treated!

What could be cuter than a sweet little junior boy camper with a red Gatorade mustache? Until he adds a milk mustache to the preexisting mustache, and it loses its charm!

If I had a dollar for every lifesaving Band-Aid I have applied today, I could pay off my mortgage! The rules are simple. It must be bleeding to warrant a Band-Aid. If actually bleeding, it will require washing with soap and water. Those are the rules. Do you want a Band-Aid or not?

Chiggers are the ailment of the day. I've had a dozen sheepish faces come see me, whispering, "Nurse Amber...I have some little bites. They are really itchy. No, I don't want you to look at them. They are "down there."

Me to a camper, "I can't explain why chiggers like your private parts like they do, they just do!!! Here's some anti-itch medicine, and remember, you can't shower or swim too much."

One senior boy quarantined for possible strep. Temperature of 102.4 and chills. Heading to urgent care in the morning—again. Now, praying for limited exposure!

I'm whipped!

I'm tired, but still fighting the good fight.

NURSE AMBER-OUT!

Day 4 of Burnt Cabin Youth Camp! (Exclamation point is back!)

I'm starting to get Yelling Guy. These kids do need to be screamed at—and often. I'm even noticing a slight frown on Kumbaya Girl. Reality hurts, don't it girl.

Wednesday's the WORST day of camp! Lunch today—some kind of recycled hotdog matter, red punch (because it looks so good on the lips of campers), rubbery Rice Crispy bars, and my favorite, the brown glob of something. Wednesday is the worst because it's been three days away from home, three days of eating strange food that I pray people don't typically eat! And, three days until I feel my bed at home. Three days can seem like eternity on Wednesday at camp.

I've had a version of this conversation multiple times today, "Nurse Amber, I don't feel good, my belly hurts."

Me, "What's going on? Do you need to vomit?"

"No."

"Have you pooped since you came to camp?"

Silence.

"I think you need to eat some fruit, drink more water, and take a trip to the salad bar. Then you need to spend some time sitting on the pot. We've had this conversation before!"

Camper replies, "I can't poop at camp. They're too many people in my cabin. It's so embarrassing."

"I have no doubt you can hold your bathroom essentials until school is out when you are home, but buddy we're here for the whole week so that won't fly. Go poop!"

"Can I use your bathroom?"

Me with a sigh of defeat, "Yes. I'll walk to the mess hall and back."

My bathroom has been blown up four times today!

I've been doing this church camp nurse gig for a while. This is my 11th, I don't know, maybe 12th year. I have established some camp/life rules along the way. The older campers know them well. The younger ones will figure them out!

1. If there is NO VISIBLE blood you do NOT get/need a Band-Aid.

2. If the Band-Aid criteria is met, then there will be washing with soap and water PRIOR to the application of said Band-Aid (This practice greatly reduces the need for Band-Aids and probably hurts the company's stock price!)

3. If you complain to me about a bellyache we will talk about the water you have not had enough of, and we will talk about POOP and the last time you produced any! It's a nurse thing.

4. When it's HOT outside—and it's ALWAYS hot at summer camp—you will need to drink more water. You cannot SWEAT DR. PEPPER!! I say this every year.

5. At camp, and in life, you ALWAYS have a choice! You can do what I say and be HAPPY, or you can do what I say and be SAD!

Not one of the five rules, but still an observation. The general bug bites, ticks, chiggers, and sand fleas must build character in some way. There can be no other purpose for them, I am sure!

P.S. Why do kids keep giving me teeth? I have had three more junior boys give me teeth they have wiggled out of their tiny heads! I'm NOT the Tooth Fairy, but close to now having a complete set of teeth for the week.

NURSE AMBER-OUT

DAY 5 at Burnt Cabin Youth Camp

In addition to Church Camp this week here at Burnt Cabin on beautiful Lake Tenkiller, we are also hosting a tick and chigger festival! These kids are eaten up! I gave my bug spray speech this morning, so I hope more bug spray has been applied! I have purchased EVERY bottle of Tecnu Itch Spray® that can be found in Cherokee county!

We started this day with a couple of trips to urgent care and two positive cases of strep throat. Hopefully we are all done with that!

Okay, I've trampled over most of this camp and seen no poison ivy, but today, a senior boy comes in covered with the rash up to his knees. I thought we had enough with chiggers and ticks, but this kid must have gone into the deep woods to find yet another discomfort. I covered him in cortisone cream and calamine lotion, while firmly reminding him to not scratch it, touch it, or think about it—or it will spread.

Camper, "Nurse Amber, I have a tick in my armpit!"

I'm thinking: Where's your counselor. They magically disappear at these times every year. Yelling Guy should be able to shout the tick into submission.

Me, "Well, let me see it."

Camper, "You can look at it but don't touch it or pull on it or do anything that will make it hurt."

Me, "Oh, honey. Hurt is what I do. How do you think I'm going to get that out without touching it at all?"

Camper, "I'm not really sure, maybe you should take me to the hospital, or I'll just wait until Saturday, and my mom can take it out when I get home."

"Trust me," I say. "Your mom's not going to want to do that."

Camper, "My momma loves me."

I'm thinking that's hard to believe.

Me, "Do you think any girl is gonna want to go to the big social with a guy that has a bug living in his armpit?"

Camper, "I guess I'll let you get it out or—maybe I should find out if she hates bugs, first!"

Lyme disease or love? The struggle is real!

Watched two intermediates whacking each other with ping pong paddles. Would like to slap some rear ends with those paddles. Fortunately, Yelling Guy is there. Go get'em, Yelling Guy!

Oh no! I think to myself. A second camper with poison ivy— a senior girl this time. Again, I've seen no poison ivy except from the senior boy that confessed he went into the woods. Time to have a talk about the birds and the bees—and the ticks and the fleas. Both rashes below the knees, so I can only hope we were just holding hands in the woods. Time will tell, but I'm praying hard.

NURSE AMBER-OUT

<u>Day 6 at Burnt Cabin Youth Camp!</u>

It's the last full day at camp! Sunburns, ticks and chiggers are still the theme for the day. Walking through the mess hall at breakfast, I had a large bag of anti-itch wipes. I gave some to several junior campers, who were all eager. It's like Christmas in June when they get something from Nurse Amber. I pass by a group of very manly senior boy campers.

"Anyone need anti-itch wipes?" I ask. "Anyone?"

Multiple sets of eyes looking down.

One pipes up, "I have a few bites on my leg, I'd like one."

I frown, "Why don't you just admit you ALL have a crotch full of chigger bites. Take a wipe!"

I dispensed 12-13 wipes in less than 30 seconds!

No more "poison ivy" outbreaks from the deep woods, and the two that were exposed still only have it below the knees. I wish all young love was restricted to holding hands in the woods—and only getting a rash below the knees. Life would be simpler.

Three junior boys come to my cabin. One of them had a pretty good gash on his knee. The other two were there for moral support. The injured boy may need stitches. He's a country kid and more concerned about getting blood on the new shorts his mom had bought him than the potential stitches he needs. I hate to tell him his mom will probably want to burn everything that makes it back from camp.

How does one child (who is NOT playing softball) manage to get hit with the ball three times during one game!?! It's not the first time I've seen this kid. He is like a conductor of unfortunate mishaps and accidents.

Kumbaya Girl lost it today. She's finally learned that talking kindly to children will only take you so far. Some intermediate boy pushed her buttons. She grabs him, wrestles him to the ground, and sits on him for a moment, while a host of other intermediates watch in disbelief.

"What are you looking at!?!" she screams to the bewildered onlookers.

"Nothing to see here," I calmly say, to disperse the mob. When they fail to move fast enough, I add, "Or I'll call Yelling Guy."

They move. I love Yelling Guy. Even the threat of him achieves results. Spend the next half hour with Kumbaya Girl convincing her everything will be all right.

"I don't know if I want children after this week," she weeps.

"Your own kids will be different," I try to affirm by lying blatantly to her. "You'll be a great mom."

Is lying *always* bad? I have a difficult time with this question. I believe in honesty—at least in theory—but, if every potential parent knew their offspring would turn out to be a stinky, snotty, sarcastic, and snarky intermediate there would be no more people on earth. I rationalize that it's okay for her to believe her children might be different. It perpetuates the human race. She'll learn the truth in time. Kumbaya Girl made it through the day. Somehow, Yelling Guy seems almost normal to us by this time of the week.

I can't figure Yelling Guy out. He scolds and shouts at kids all week, yet they seem to really like him by the end of camp. Kumbaya Girl has done everything to endear herself to campers, but they have utterly defeated her.

I removed one wad of gum from a camper's hair.

Camper, "I don't know how it got there."

Me, "I guess we forgot the rule about no food in the bunkhouse or gum at camp?"

"It wasn't me," the camper reflex lies.

What? Do I look like I was born yesterday? I cut out the bubble gum with a judgmental scowl and a lack of any surgical precision. She'll have a few weeks to grow that mess out. Point made.

Me to another camper, "Hey, missy, why are you wearing your coat? It's 94 degrees outside."

Camper whispers, "I have sweat rings on the armpits of my shirt so I put my coat on so nobody can see it!"

Still shaking my head! Can't argue her logic, but feel I should.

We are all tired and sweaty and wearing our cleanest dirty clothes. We're covered in bug bites, but happily filled with the comradery of the week. Ready to go home—but not ready to go home, if you can follow my logic.

I had my bathroom blown up two more times, the second incident required a PLUNGER and a PRAYER!

SO, SO, TIRED! Ready for some sleep! It's been a good week but I'm worn out and sick of being a hot sweaty mess!
NURSE AMBER-OUT

Last day at Burnt Cabin Youth Camp

Been looking forward to this day since day one, but now it's so sad. These whiny, dirty, snot-nosed kids have a place in my heart that's hard to explain. Won't miss the counselors as much—at least until I get home. One final camp tradition. A pile of unclaimed clothes that would outfit a battalion. Any junior underwear is hopelessly lost and will not be claimed even when we show the kid the name tag their mom had carefully sewn into it. Oh well, it wouldn't be camp without surplus clothes. At least we didn't leave any anti-itch medicine unused.

NURSE AMBER-OUT (For good, but will be looking forward to next year soon.)

THE END

KELLY'S QUEST

She seemed out of place at the State Amateur Women's Golf Championship, although she looked comfortable and natural standing on the first tee. Kelly was easily twice the age of most her opponents. She stood there with a disarming smile camouflaging a fierce competitive spirit. Kelly was not here to compete, however, as much as to remember. Cedar Ridge Country Club was a tough, but fair course that hosted the 1983 United States Women's Open Championship. More importantly to Kelly, it was one of the golf courses on her list.

The college girl she was paired with that day was not yet twenty, while Kelly had already conquered fifty years of life. The college girl was tall, athletic, and looked as if she had been raised at a country club. Kelly, by contrast, stood barely taller than five foot and liked the country more than a club. Her slight stature and matronly appearance hid the fact that she had been a four-year starter as point guard in her college years, named to the all-conference team three years, while helping two other teammates become All-Americans. Kelly never touched a golf club until she met her husband. It became her game...her family's game. Even after two children, she continued to play and improve. She could have been one of the best women players in the state, but family was first, and Kelly was content to play recreationally as the family grew. It was only after that one life-changing day when golf became more than a game—it became her quest.

By the fourteenth hole, Kelly conceded her match to the college girl, but indicated she intended to finish the round. Finishing the round, Kelly would explain, had become her obsession. The college girl thought she understood and offered to play the last four holes with her. The girl planned to play competitively through college before getting on with life. Kelly listened intently and smiled often as she would give reassuring nods to the girl's ambitions. Soon the conversation turned to Kelly, but talking about herself was something she did not like to do. The girl gently pressed her, however.

"Cedar Ridge is a course on my list," Kelly confessed.

"List?" the girl replied.

Kelly nodded and smiled politely as she explained. The girl listened attentively—they always did. Kelly's story was one of great tragedy, and her redemption was playing all of the courses on her list. The list was long and covered states from Florida to Arizona. Kelly was hesitant to reveal her list, but people were always genuinely interested, and she would tell the many tales of her journey and what she hoped to find at the end.

"I'm down to three," Kelly smiled. "The last is Emerald Falls—in Tulsa. That was the last course—the last memory."

The girl, who had pleasantly and eagerly listened to the story, suddenly turned pale as they walked up the eighteenth hole. The story—the quest had fascinated the college girl, but now the girl felt anxious and uneasy.

Kelly had been a mother too long not to notice. "What's wrong?"

The girl stopped at the edge of the green and looked around as if searching for an escape. Finally, the girl swallowed hard before revealing, "Emerald Falls closed."

This revelation was met with a silence amplifying the placid calm of the golf course.

"Closed?" Kelly eventually clarified.

"This spring," the girl replied. "I think they went bankrupt. It hasn't been open for months, and I've heard the bank plans to sell the course into lots."

The news felt like a crushing weight pressing down on her very soul. For six years, Kelly had kept some sense of sanity by pursuing her list. She had good experiences and bad. Some great golf courses and some that thought too highly of themselves, but all had taken her closer to her goal. Through it all, she had persevered and played them all. Now, three were left, and the last was to be Emerald Falls. The final golf course on her list had to be Emerald Falls. If Kelly had learned anything on her personal journey, it had been to keep her emotions to herself. The news that Emerald Falls was bankrupt was devastating, but she could keep her countenance in front of the girl. She could disguise this overwhelming disappointment.

"Maybe they'll reopen it," Kelly managed to say.

"I sure hope so," the girl consoled, although Kelly can tell by the girl's reaction that all hope is lost.

Kelly said her goodbyes to the tournament officials and wished the girl good luck in her next match. She retreated to her car and felt some comfort in the loneliness of its hot interior. She felt like crying, but had shed too many tears to do so now. She called her husband to share the bad news. She could sense the disappointment in his voice, because it had been his quest too. He knew what to say and believed it was his job to give her some hope, although she could tell by his voice that he had no more idea about how to finish than she did.

The drive home was lonely, as they all had been since that day. Kelly learned to adapt in many ways, but checking the courses off her list had been the best therapy. What she hated most was dealing with the well-wishing people that could never understand, no matter how hard they tried. She had learned to cope. She developed the ability to deflect their probing questions. She managed to survive to this point, although there were plenty of times she doubted she could. She hated when people would say, "I know what you're going through." They meant well, but they could never know, they could never understand. The golf course knew, the golf courses understood her and her quest. Emerald Falls had always been the goal. It was always meant to be the final chapter to her story.

As summer edged toward autumn, Kelly dutifully played the two courses left on her list with her husband. She pointed out all the things she had seen—all the things she remembered. He understood, but there was still that foreboding truth—Emerald Falls was closed. The last course was gone. It was early October when they made the drive to the now out-of-business golf course. The Emerald Falls Golf Club still showed pictures on their defunct website to tantalize her, but as they drove past the entrance to the course, it looked more like something from beyond the apocalypse. Through the dirty windows, there were still remnants of hangers and vestiges of racks that once held golf apparel and equipment. The property had been closed only a short while, but it seemed stuck in time. Kelly remembered the vibrancy of the place on her previous visit from only a few years back that now seemed a lifetime ago. The hope and expectations vanished that day, much like happiness seemed to disappear from her life.

Her husband, however, was resilient and a problem solver. He did not see any barrier as insurmountable. The couple survived the past six years by living with a simple precept, "One Shot at a Time." Those words had not only been instructions on how to play the game of golf, but had become their mission statement for life. He was a man who held high expectations for himself and others. He did not accept excuses and would not exempt himself from completing his wife's goal. It had been his idea for them to take a five-iron and a couple of balls to the remnants of Emerald Falls and walk every step.

It was a cloudy but warm autumn day, the kind of day where the humidity hung on everything and covered the overgrown cart paths with a glimmering glaze of moisture. They waded through ankle high grass now filled with weeds and neglect. Homes facing the one-time golf course were still manicured, and a few residents even put some effort into mowing parts of the course. It was a quiet walk through the lonely and vacant relic of a golf course. Kelly pointed out features of the course and remembered the last time she had been here. A few of the neighbors stared at their trespassing, but none approached, and they walked their path unmolested until the last and final hole.

"What are you doing here?" a man with a nice home on the right side of the eighteenth fairway demanded.

This is a confrontation Kelly had feared all day. She did not have authorization to be on this land and did not even know who to contact to get permission.

"Let me handle this," her husband said, as he turned to face the man.

Kelly nodded and stood by herself in the middle of what was the final hole at Emerald Falls remembering that day. She knew the conversation her husband would have with the agitated neighbor. Her husband would tell the man about her purpose for being there. The neighbor would understand—people always did, but she was tired of their sympathy. She stood alone in the fairway and stared at the place where the final green had been. She had her five-iron in hand and planned to hit a shot to the place where her hope had once ended.

Her husband stood at the edge of the yard. She believed they were talking about the fate of the bankrupt golf course. She felt awkward standing alone but would rather be with her thoughts than have to endure the conversation one more time. He would tell the man about their son—their only son, their pride and joy—who had played here six years earlier. It had been the All-State tournament. Their son played well that day. There was always room for improvement, but that mattered for nothing now. The world was inviting him to a great future. He had a scholarship to the school of his dreams. He had been recruited by many universities across the nation but chose the University of Oklahoma, where he had sat in the south end zone for home football games since he could walk. Kelly had watched every shot of every tournament her son ever played, including this last one.

He would explain it had been a hot and humid July day when his son walked off this course six years ago. The boy had driven himself knowing his mother would follow. On the drive back, he had passed out, and the pickup truck he drove smashed into the pillar of an interstate bridge. Everything changed—forever. Kelly, following her son in a separate vehicle, had been the first to arrive at the horrifying scene. The accident seemed surreal, but even in her dreams now, she would wake up to the fact that her nightmare was a reality.

Her husband had taken the loss as hard as she had. She worried about him, more than she did about herself, many times. It took weeks and then months that turned into years for them to realize life would never be the same, but that life did go on. Their faith had been their salvation. She heard people say more times than she could remember, "No parent should ever have to bury a child." They were well-intentioned, but those words could never be comprehended the way she had been forced to learn them.

Her husband returned from telling the story and she asked, "Well?"

"He said to take our time," her husband replied. "He said he understood."

She smiled at her husband. It had become their little joke when people said they understood, because they knew few could or would want to understand what they had gone through.

Her husband continued, "He said they wanted to find a new owner and reopen the course, but at the last neighborhood association meeting he heard the bank was going to sell the course to developers to build houses."

Kelly looks around at the overgrown course before saying, "That's a shame. It was a nice layout."

Her husband nodded.

"So, we can hit the shot?" Kelly asked.

"Well, I guess that's what we came for," he replied.

Her husband took his five-iron and a ball. With a smooth swing, the ball started a little right before drawing back toward the target.

"Good shot," she encouraged.

"Got it a little on the toe," he complained.

She smirked and shook her head so slightly it was not noticeable in response to her perfectionist husband's commentary about his own game. He was always looking to do better. She walked up a few yards and found her spot where she dropped her ball. Before hitting her shot, she said, "Kyle hit a wedge from here. He put it seven feet right."

She swung her club and made solid contact. The ball was on a good line, but it didn't really matter to her. This was the shot she wanted to hit and the result was inconsequential.

"Nice shot," her husband announced.

"I think it would have found the green," she stoically assessed.

As they walk toward the place where the eighteenth green used to be, Kelly says, "This isn't too bad. I mean finishing all these courses this way."

"What do you mean, hon?"

Kelly shrugged, "I wanted to play all the courses he played, and did. It seems right that this one kept me from completing my goal—at least the way I wanted. Kyle's life was incomplete and something about it just seems right."

"Maybe," her husband agrees.

"This course is gone, but its memory lives on," Kelly explains. "I don't ever want to forget, and I don't want others to forget, either. Kyle's memory lives on—his spirit lives on. I like to think he would tell me life goes on. It hasn't been easy, but life does go on."

"It does."

On the place where the last green had been, Kelly points to where the pin had been that day. She and her husband carefully walk the ground where their son took some of the last steps of his too short life. She never realized when she watched him reach down to take his ball out of the cup that it would be the last time. She wishes she could freeze that moment and keep it forever. Everything was so routine that day. There would be many more finishes, and she planned to be at all of them for her son.

The couple traced the steps where the scorer's tent had been. Kelly rarely cries, but tears up slightly as she follows the path to where she had watched her son climb into that pickup for his drive home. She remembers thinking how hard it was going to be to have him leave for college. It never occurred to her this place would be the end—the last moments she had with her son and all of his promise.

"You never know do you?" she states.

"About what?" her husband asks.

"About life," she explains. "You think things are permanent, but we're all temporary. Everything can change in an instant."

"I think we've learned that," he replies.

Kelly looks around the overgrown asphalt where the parking lot had been before saying, "Let's go home. It's over—but—it's really never over. I've completed my quest. That's what I set out to do."

"Do you feel better?" he asks.

Kelly shakes her head and answers, "Not particularly, but I feel like I accomplished something. Kyle would have liked that." She smiles at her husband before saying, "You can only take it one shot at a time."

"One shot at a time," he repeats.

Kelly's quest was over, but they understood their journey would never really be complete.

THE END

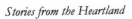

AUTHOR'S NOTES

I believe the drama of life happens around us all of the time, if we can only find the perspective to see it. The following notes are intended to give readers some insights into the origins of these short stories. I hope you enjoyed *Stories from the Heartland*.

JOSEPHINE KNEW—This story is very personal to me. My youngest brother was adopted when he was an infant. He did not meet his biological mother until he was nearly forty years old. I've always appreciated the memories I've had with my brothers. It was never in our consciousness that he had any different background. The story tries to capture some of the experience of discovering something about yourself that you did not know was there.

GRANDMA'S HATCHET—Sometimes family stories are passed down for no other reason than entertainment and nostalgia. I've heard this story told by family members many times. I have no idea about the accuracy of the events, but it was always an entertaining image of a job half-done.

CLETUS CALLAWAY—Cletus Callaway is not a character I have ever known, yet I believe I have encountered many with his ability to spend more time on schemes than productive work. The twist at the end can probably be attributed to a myriad of "preacher stories" I've heard in my life.

A CONFUSING END—I'm not sure one can accurately chronicle the thought process of dementia. It seems some personality traits become exaggerated, while sometimes the individual changes so dramatically, they do not seem like the same person. In this story, the character retreats into their past trying to find some safety from their confusing end.

THE FATHER ROAD—This story is based on a compilation of vacations taken with my dad when I was a preteen. The events are not really embellished and some have been omitted to protect the innocent and the guilty.

THE LETTER—The letter that begins this story actually exists, and I have quoted it with very little editing. It hung in my grandfather's office for many years. We always wondered what happened to the boys in the letter. It appeared they disappeared, as so many did during the Civil War, shortly after the letter was written. This story envisions what might have happened to the boys, but deals more with the aftermath of a mother they left behind.

THE SANCTUARY—The original version of this story was told by a librarian during a job interview. I thought it a particularly powerful example of the challenges that surround us every day. Libraries really are sanctuaries, and librarians in our society are often doing as much social work as research. And yes, the woman got the job.

CONFESSIONS OF A SALESMAN—Working in my family's furniture business from age sixteen to thirty-five taught me a lot about consumer behavior, human psychology, and humor. The manipulative furniture shopper in this story may seem a little too over-the-top, but a version of her actually existed along with many, many other interesting characters.

JACK FULLER'S UNDERSTANDING—This story again beckons back to my retail selling experiences. The real Jack Fuller was much more dynamic and community oriented than I was able to describe in a short story. The part of the tale about his experiences in the war and his modesty about that one event was very real. This story reminds me that extraordinary people are around us all of the time, if we will only recognize it.

THE TOMBSTONE—This may be the most accurately recorded story in this collection. There really is a tombstone of my grandfather's first wife. I discovered it a few months ago, and it really caused me to think about how events dramatically affect present and future generations.

TALE OF TWO CATS—I have an indoor cat and an outdoor cat. They both want what the other has. They have taught me a lot about myself and others.

THE WOMAN THEY CALLED MOM—I have experienced several women in my life that have sacrificed for kids that were not their own. My wife has a co-worker who is fairly young, but already dedicates much of her personal resources to help make a better life for others. This story tries to show that being kind does have its own benefit.

A TITANIC DESTINY—This is a fanciful story about what a person might could do, if they knew exactly what was going to happen. I've had a long fascination with the Titanic tragedy and much of my earlier writings are in that era. Time traveling heroes are not my genre, but I had fun with this story anyway.

THE BOOK COVER—A good friend of mine, Clarence Prevost, has a minority background, which is diverse from my own. We have become friends and discovered we have many things from our childhood in common. This is his story about growing up with segregation. I purposefully try to create a character with a sense of nostalgia that is familiar to many middle-class Americans, while hiding the character's ethnicity. The theme of the story is how hurtful we can unintentionally be and that we all have very similar experiences regardless of our backgrounds.

THE GENERATIONS—This is a story that very accurately depicts a scene on the fourth hole of the Donald Ross designed Elk's Club in Southern Pines, North Carolina between my father, my grandfather, and me. I had the privilege of knowing all of my grandparents well, and greatly benefited by their support.

THE PREACHER—This story occurs in the same era when many of my historical fiction novels are set. I thought about making this into a longer work, but liked the moral dilemma presented in the short story, and the soul-searching twist the preacher provides at the end.

THE BULLY—This story does not refer to any real person or events, but tries to capture the anxiety most middle school students go through. The theme is simple; do not judge people before you get to know them. I've found many of my best friends in life were not necessarily people I immediately gravitated to, but that I grew to know.

THE OLD PEAR TREE—This story came to me while looking at the old pear tree in my backyard. The tree had been bent and shaped by the years, just like most people are a product of their experiences.

THE DIARY OF NURSE AMBER—Though not as historically relevant, gripping, or as important as the *Diary of Ann Frank*, this humorous chronicling of camp tales has its own dramas. I've been wanting to write down some camp stories for years, and decided telling those stories through the real Nurse Amber's perspective would be a great way. This story takes some of Nurse Amber's social media posts from several years and enhances them with other stories that could only happen at a week of camp.

KELLY'S QUEST—I have known several people who have lost a child too early in life. Kyle Lewis's parents are the closest perspective I've had to that kind of tragedy. *Kelly's Quest* is the story of a mom and dad trying to cope and make some sense out of a life catastrophe. They have to deal with a host of emotions and challenges that only a parent in that circumstance could understand. In the end, they try to carry on with life, make some sense out of the senseless, and remember.

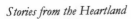

If you enjoyed

Stories from the Heartland

Look for these other Bob Perry novels:

The Broken Statue
Mimosa Lane
Brothers of the Cross Timber
Guilt's Echo
Lydie's Ghost
The Nephilim Code
Return from Wrath
WOBS: The Wisdom Of Bob
For the Greater Good
For the Greater Good: Abigail's Story
For the Greater Good: Redemption
The Beast of Chatsworth

www.bobp.biz